Lucy Hooper

The Lady's Book of Flowers and Poetry

to which are added a botanical introduction, a complete floral dictionary and a

chapter on plants in rooms

Lucy Hooper

The Lady's Book of Flowers and Poetry
to which are added a botanical introduction, a complete floral dictionary and a chapter on plants in rooms

ISBN/EAN: 9783337271268

Printed in Europe, USA, Canada, Australia, Japan

Cover: Foto ©Andreas Hilbeck / pixelio.de

More available books at **www.hansebooks.com**

THE

LADY'S BOOK

OF

FLOWERS AND POETRY;

TO WHICH ARE ADDED

A BOTANICAL INTRODUCTION,

A COMPLETE FLORAL DICTIONARY

AND

A CHAPTER ON PLANTS IN ROOMS.

EDITED BY LUCY HOOPER.

PHILADELPHIA
CLAXTON, REMSEN & HAFFELFINGER,
819 & 821 MARKET STREET.
1868.

PREFACE.

IN presenting the "BOOK OF FLOWERS AND POETRY" to our readers, we would observe that much pains have been taken to render its contents as varied and interesting as the limits of such a work will allow. It will be found to contain a copious Floral Dictionary, with many of the Eastern significations not generally known. To these are added remarks on the cultivation of flowers, and a simple abstract of Botany compiled from the works of our best writers.

To the selections from our own native poets we turn with pride and pleasure; not the less is our gratification in tendering in this place, our acknowledgments to the distinguished writers who have assisted us by original articles from their pens. We would particularly mention Mr. CHARLES F. HOFFMAN, Mrs. EMMA C. EMBURY, and Mr. WM. CULLEN BRYANT. Nor would we forget the beautiful effusion of Mrs. BALMANNO, and the graceful verses of Miss HUNTINGTON, names less known, because those who own them, are content to shed the odor of their talents, only round the circle of their own immediate friends.

L. Y

TO

I HAVE bound thee a garland of fresh blooming roses,
  The brightest, the fairest that nature can yield,
The sigh that I've breathed, on its bosom reposes,
  The tear that I've dropped, by its leaves is con-
    cealed.

Then take the frail tribute thou loved one and wear it,
  At least till it withers, 't will bloom but a day,
And if, from your forehead, all faded you tear it,
  Think once on the giver — then cast it away.

INTRODUCTION

TO THE

LADY'S BOOK OF FLOWERS AND POETRY

" Who does not love a flower,
　　Its hues are taken from the light
　　Which summer's suns fling pure and bright,
　　In scattered and prismatic hues,
　　That smile and shine in dropping dews ;
　　Its fragrance from the sweetest air,
　　Its form from all that 's light and fair,
　　Who does not love a flower."

BRAINARD.

THE above lines express too fully the natural sentiments of the heart, to need any formal remarks from us on the beauties of flowers. Dear to all are these favorite children of Nature, smiling out from the solitary nook, and blooming amid high and rugged cliffs. Linked with many a fond association, may be the simplest flower, from the "*rosemary*," which is for "remembrance," to the wild flower of the fields, which brings back to us a thousand bright recollections of sunny and rambling hours, when a fair unclouded future

lay before us, and even a flower could borrow most
brilliant colors from the imagination. Who does not
recall with pleasure

> " The flowers, the many flowers
> > That all along the smiling valley grew,
>
> While the sun lay for hours
> > Kissing from off their drooping lids the dew."

Oh! there is something in such remembrances that
even in hours of depression and sorrow, can brighten
the dim eye and ease the wearied mind, bringing a fund
of innocent and pure enjoyment. Flowers are types
of our brightest hopes, they are emblems of joy, they
have been even called " the alphabet of angels." And
the harmony of their colors, the variety of their forms,
the profusion with which they are scattered over
every solitary place, make us consider them as fragrant
gems of the earth, beautiful ministers of winged and
spiritual thoughts. In the language of poetry, they
are called by one of our American poets Professor
Longfellow,

> " The flowers, so blue and golden,
> > STARS, that in Earth's firmament do shine.

> " Wondrous truths, and manifold as wondrous,
> > God hath written in those stars above ;
>
> But not less in the bright flowerets under us,
> > Stands the revelation of his love.

"Bright and glorious is that revelation,
    Written all over this great world of ours,
  Making evident our own creation,
    In these stars of Earth — these golden flowers

" And the Poet, faithful and far-seeing,
    Sees, alike in stars and flowers, a part
  Of the self-same, universal being
    Which is throbbing in his brain and heart.

" Gorgeous flowerets in the sunlight shining
    Blossoms flaunting in the eye of day ;
  Tremulous leaves, with soft and silver lining
    Buds that open only to decay.

" Brilliant hopes, all woven in gorgeous tissues.
    Flaunting gayly in the golden light ;
  Large desires, with most uncertain issues,
    Tender wishes, blossoming at night.

" Every where about us are they glowing,
    Some like stars, to tell us Spring is born ;
  Others, their blue eyes with tears o'erflowing,
    Stand like Ruth amid the golden corn. "

After so beautiful an apostrophe to Flowers, we pre
sent our Book with renewed confidence to the readers
for whom it is intended. That amid its many blossoms
they may discover some fair and fragrant flower,
which may bring pleasant images, and among its poet-

ical sentiments, find some favored selection which may address itself to their memories, is the wish of the compiler. That they may find it a mystic "Book"—a faithful ally in the cause of Flora, till they acquire proficiency in the "language of flowers," is sincerely hoped. For this purpose, much care has been used in the selection of the different meanings, and leaving our labors at present, we hope the Book we offer for the perusal will be considered

> "As a soft chain of spoken flowers
> And airy gems,

by our fair and intelligent readers

L. H

MANAGEMENT OF PLANTS IN ROOMS.

PERHAPS a few hints on the management of plants in rooms, may not be unacceptable to our readers. We, therefore, extract from Paxton's Magazine of Botany, the following observations :—

"Hints on the general management of plants are attended with considerable difficulty ; every genus requiring some little variation, both in soil, water, and general treatment. If the room where the plants are intended to be placed, is dark and close, but few will ever thrive in it; if, on the contrary, it is light and airy, with the windows in suitable aspect to receive the sun, plants will do nearly as well as in a greenhouse. If observed to suffer, the effects may be traced to these causes, either want of proper light and air—injudicious watering—filthiness collected on the leaves—or being potted in unsuitable soil.

" 1. *Want of proper light and air*, is perhaps the most essential point of any to be considered ; for, however well all other requisites are attended to, a deficiency of these will always cause the plant to grow weak and sickly. Let them always be placed as near the light as they can conveniently stand and receive as much air as can be admitted when the weather will allow. Those persons who have no other place than the house to keep them in, will find that they derive immense advantage from being, during fine weather in spring or autumn, turned out of doors in the evening, and taken in again in the morning, the night-dews contributing greatly to their health and vigor.

"2. *Injudicious watering* does more injury to plants in rooms than we imagine. To prevent the soil ever having an appearance of dryness is an object of importance in the estimation of very many ; they, therefore water to such an excess that the mould becomes sodden, and the roots perish. Ohers, to avoid this evil, give scarcely water enough to sustain life. This, however, is by no means so common a practice ; for, in general, if anything appears to be the matter with the plant large doses of water are immediately resorted to, for an infallible restorative. This overplus of water wil. show its bad effects by the very dark color, and flabby disposition of the leaves ; but if the plant receives too little water, its leaves will turn yellow and eventually die.

"The best plan is, to always allow the soil in the pot to have the appearance of dryness (but never sufficient to make the plant flag), before a supply of water is given, which should then be pretty copious ; but always empty it out of the pan or feeder, in which the pot stands, as soon as the soil is properly drained. The water used for the purpose ought always to be

made about the same temperature as the room in which
the plants grow; never use it fresh from the pump,
either let it stand in a room all night, or take off the
chill by a little warm water, otherwise the growth of
the plants will be much checked.

" 3. *Extraneous matter collected on the leaves* may
either arise from insects or dust ; the former may be
speedily remedied, by placing the plants under a hand
glass, or anything that is convenient, and burning some
tobacco until they become well enveloped in the smoke ;
and the latter may be removed by occasionally wash-
ing them on the head with pure water, either by means
of a syringe, the nose of a watering pan, or with a
sponge, when the dust still adheres.

Bulbs of most sorts flourish in rooms with less care
than most other plants. Hyacinths should be planted
in autumn. Fill the pots with light rich soil, and plant
the bulbs so shallow that nearly half the bulb stands
above the soil, place the pots in the open air, and
cover them six or eight inches with rotten bark. During spring, take them out as they are wanted to bring
into flower, and set them in the window of a warm
room, where they will be exposed to the sun. When
the leaves begin to decay after flowering, give them no
water, when the leaves are dead, take them out of the
soil, and lay them in an airy situation for planting.

" If grown in water-glasses, they require to be placed
in a light airy situation, and the water must be changed
every three or four days.

GARDENS, WREATHS, &c.

LEGENDS OF FLOWERS.

LUCY HOOPER.

The following lines refer to some of the old fanciful ideas attached to the opening of flowers. In the Romish church such events were carefully noted down, and every flower blossoming on a Saint's day was considered to bloom in honor of that saint.

Oh gorgeous tales, in the days of old,
  Were linked with the opening flowers,
As if in their fairy urns of gold,
  Beat human hearts like ours.
The nuns in their cloister, sad and pale,
  As they watched soft buds expand,
On their glowing petals traced a tale
  Or legend of holy Land.
Brightly to them did thy snowy leaves,
  For the sainted Mary shine,
As they twined for her forehead vestal wreaths
  Of thy white buds, Cardamine!

The Crocus shone when the fields were bare
  With a gay rejoicing smile;

But the hearts that answered Love's tender prayer
  Grew brightened with joy the while.
Of the coming spring, and the summer's light,
  To others that flower might say,
But the lover welcomed the herald bright,
  Of the glad St. Valentine's day.
The Crocus was hailed as a happy flower,
  And the holy Saint that day
Poured out on the Earth their golden shower,
  To light his votaries' way.

—

On the day of St. George, the brave St. George
  To merry England dear,
By field and by fell, and by mountain gorge,
  Shone Hyacinths blue and clear.
Lovely and prized was their purple light,
  And 'twas said in ancient story,
That their fairy bells rung out at night,
  A peal to old England's glory.
And sages read in the azure hue,
  Of the flowers so widely known,
That by white sail spread over Ocean's blue,
  Should the Empire's right be shown.

—

And thou, of faithful memory,
  St. John, thou "shining light,"
Beams not a burning torch for thee,
  The scarlet Lychnis bright·

While holy Mary at thy shrine,
  Another pure flower blooms,
Welcome to thee with news divine,*
  The lily's faint perfume.
Proudly its stately head it rears,
  Arrayed in virgin white,
So Truth, amid a world of tears,
  Doth shine with vestal light.

—

And thou, whose opening buds were and
  A Saviour's cross beside,
We hail thee, Passion Flower alone
  Sacred to Christ who died.
No image of a mortal love,
  May thy bright blossoms be
Linked with a passion far above,
  A Saviour's agony.
All other flowers are pale and dim,
  All other gifts are loss,
We twine thy matchless buds for him
  Who died on holy Cross.

* The Lily blooms about Annunciation day

2*

THE PAINTED CUP.*

WILLIAM C. BRYANT.

THE fresh savannahs of the Sangamore
Here rise in gentle swells, and the long grass
Is mixed with rustling hazels. Scarlet tufts
Are glowing in the green, like flakes of fire;
The wanderers of the prairie know them well,
And call that brilliant flower the painted cup.
Now if thou art a poet, tell me not
That these bright chalices were tinted thus
To hold the dew for fairies, when they meet
On moonlight evenings in the hazel bowers,
And dance till they are thirsty. Call not up,
Amid thy fresh and virgin solitude,
The faded fancies of an elder world,
But leave these scarlet cups to spotted moths
Of June, and glistening flies, and humming-birds,
To drink from, when on all these boundless lawns
The morning sun looks hot. Or let the wind

---

* The Painted Cup or *Euchroma Coccinea* of Nuttall, is known more
generally as the Bartsia Coccinea of Linnæus, and in botanical language, is described thus : Leaves alternate, linear, cut pinnatifid, with
linear segments, bractes dilated, mostly three cleft larger than the
flowers, calyx teeth obtuse. Should our reader prefer a poetical descrip-
tion, in addition to the beautiful lines we give, we would remind them
of **J. N.** Barker's fanciful thought,

        " Harlequin Bartsia, in his painted vest
            Of green and crimson "   L H

O erturn in sport their ruddy brims, and pour
A sudden shower upon the strawberry plant,
To swell the reddening fruit that even now
Breathes a slight fragrance from the sunny slope
But thou art of a gayer fancy.   Well—
Let then the gentle Manitou of flowers,
Lingering amid the bloomy waste he loves,
Though all his swarthy worshippers are gone—
Slender and small, his rounded cheek all brown
And ruddy with the sunshine; let him come
On summer mornings when the blossoms wake,
And part with little hands the spiky grass;
And touching, with his cherry lips, the edge
Of these bright beakers, drain the gathered dew

FLOWERS.

MRS. SIGOURNEY.

I 'LL tell thee a story, sweet,
  Here, under this shady tree,
If thou 'lt keep it safe in thy faithful breast,
  I 'll whisper the whole to thee.

I had a lover, once,
  In my early, sunny hours,
A fair and fanciful youth was he,
  And he told his love in flowers.

I remember its waking sigh,
  We roam'd in a verdant spot,
And he cull'd for me a cluster bright
  Of the purple Forget-me-not.

But I was a giddy girl,
  So I toss'd it soon away,
And gathered the dandelion buds,
  And the wild grape's gadding spray.

He mark'd their blended hues,
  With a sad and reproachful eye,
For one was the symbol of thoughtless mirth,
  And one of coquetry

Yet he would not be baffled thus,
  So he brought for my crystal vase,
The rose-geranium's tender bloom,
  And the blushing hawthorn's grace.

And a brilliant and fresh bouquet,
  Of the moss-rose buds he bore —
Whose eloquent brows with dew-drops pearl'd,
  Were rich in the heart's deep lore.

I could not refuse the gift,
  Though I knew the spell it wove,
But I gave him back a snow-white bud,
  " Too young, too young to love."

Then he proffer'd a myrtle wreath,
  With damask roses fair,
And took the liberty — only think —
  To arrange it in my hair

And he prest in my yielding hand,
  The everlasting pea,
Whose questioning lips of perfume breathed,
  " Wilt thou go, wilt thou go with me ?"

Yet we were but children, still,
  And our love, though it seemed so sweet,
Was well express'd by the types it chose,
  For it pass'd away as fleet.

Though he brought the laurus-leaf,
  That changes but to die,
And the amaranth, and the evergreen,
  Yet what did they signify ?

Oft o'er his vaunted love,
  Suspicious moods had power,
So I put a French marigold in his hat,
  That gaudy jealous flower.

But the rootless passion shrank
  Like Jonah's gourd away,
Till the shivering ice-plant best might mark
  The grades of its chill decay.

And he sailed o'er the faithless sea,
To a brighter clime than ours ;—
So it faded, that fond and ficklo love,
Like its alphabet of flowers.

SONG OF THE LAST VIOLET.

EMMA. C. EMBURY.

Written immediately after receiving from a very dear friend, on Christmas day, a Violet, which had been found growing in the open air.

I'M weary of biding the pitiless blast,
I'm weary of lingering — the lone one — the *last ;*
Too long I have pined for the soft summer shower,
And the sunbeam, to waken each slumbering flower;
Too long I have drooped o'er the desolate bed,
Where my kindred so early lay withered and dead.

In vain my rich treasures of fragrance I fling,
They mingle not now with the breezes of spring ;
Too rude are the rough blasts of winter to bear
Such perfume as gladdens the soft summer air;
And the Violet, the pride of the spring-time, soon dies,
Unknown and unseen, 'neath December's dark skies.

Oh, better, far better, 't would be, could I fade
Mid the clustering locks of some pitying maid;
But I listen in vain for the echoing tread
Of the young and the gay round my verdureless bed;

And long have I wanted the hand that might save,
My tempest-bowed form from a snow-covered grave.

Thou art come!—thou art come!—ay, I know
   thee now,
By the silent step, and the thoughtful brow,
By the calm, sweet smile on the lip, which tells
Of a soul that in peace and purity dwells,
By the tenderness glassed in the depths of thine eye
I know *thou* wilt not pass the last Violet by.

LINES TO A BELLE.

FOR THE ORCHIS.

O. W. HOLMES.

YES, lady! I can ne'er forget
That once in other years we met;
Thy memory may perchance recall
A festal eve—a rose-wreathed hall,
Its taper's blaze—its mirror's glance—
Its melting song—its ringing dance—
Why in thy dream of virgin joy,
Shouldst thou recall a pallid boy?

Thine eye had other forms to seek—
Why rest upon his bashful cheek?
With other tones thy heart was stirred—
Why waste on him a gentle word?

We parted, lady! all night long
Thine ear to thrill with dance and song;
And I to weep, that I was born
A thing thou scarce would deign to scorn

And, lady, now that years have past,
My barque has reached the shore at last;
The gales that filled her ocean wing
Have chilled and shrunk thy hasty spring;
And eye to eye, and brow to brow,
I stand before thy presence now;
Thy lip is smoothed, thy voice is sweet,
Thy warm hand proffered when we meet

Nay, lady! 't is not now for me
To droop the lid, or bend the knee;
I seek thee, oh! thou dost not shun,
I speak — thou listenest like a nun;
I ask thy smile — thy lip uncurls,
Too liberal of its flashing pearls:
Thy tears — thy lashes sink again,
My Hebe turns to Magdalen!

Oh, changing youth! that evening hour
Looked down on ours, the bud, the flower
One faded in its virgin soil,
And one was nursed in tears and toil;
Thy leaves were opening one by one,
While mine were opening to the sun;

Which now can meet the cold, the storm,
With freshest leaf and hardiest form?

Ay, lady, that once haughty glance
Still wanders vainly through the dance;
And asks in vain from others' pride,
The charity thine own denied;
And as thy ripened life could learn
To smile and praise, that used to spurn.
So thy last offering on the shrine
Shall be this flattering lay of mine.

A CLUMP OF DAISIES

RICHARD DANA.

Ye daisies gay,
This fresh spring day,
Close gathered here together,
To play in the light,
To sleep all night,
To abide through the sullen weather.

Ye creatures bland,
A simple band,
Ye free ones linked in pleasure,
And linked when your forms
Stoop low in the storms,
And the rain comes down without measure.

3

When wild clouds fly
Athwart the sky,
And ghostly shadows glancing
Are darkening the gleam
Of the hurrying stream,
And your close, bright heads gayly dancing

Though dull awhile,
Again ye smile,
For, see, the warm sun breaking,
The streams going glad,
There's nothing sad,
And the small bird his song is waking.

The dew-drop sip
With dainty lip,
The sun is low descended,
And Moon, softly fall
On troop true and small,
Sky and earth in one kindly blended.

And Morning, spread
Their jewelled bed
With lights in the east sky springing.
And Brook, breathe around
Thy low murmured sound,
May they move, ye birds, to your singing,

For in thy play,
I hear them say,

Here, man, thy wisdom borrow,
        In heart be a child,
        In word, true and mild,
Hold by faith, come joy, or come sorrow.

INVOCATION TO A WREATH OF TRANSATLANTIC FLOWERS.

MRS. BALMANNO.

YE flowers that o'er the dark dread sea,
Like faded mourners come,
By your past beauty, tell to me
A tale of mine own home.
What of my Father, hardy leaf
Of Albion's bulwark tree ?—
        He lives—unharmed by age or grief,
        His emblem I to thee ;
        His step is firm, his eye is bright,
        His accents clear and strong
        As when, thy childhood to delight,
        He raised the joyous song.
What of my Mother, lovely rose,
Speak—for my tears are nigh ?--
        Look on the stream that placid flows,
        And the unclouded sky :
        For these in heaven's own language show
        Her spirit unto thine :

The stream — her life's pure course below
The sky — her trust divine.
What of my Sister, tell, oh tell,
Thou gentlest forest-child,
Thou fairy-nun, meek violet-bell,
So modest, sweet, and mild ? —

Think of my opening blossoms, when
They first adorn the lea —
The ring-dove in her leafy glen,
Or hive-crowned honey-bee.

What of my Brothers — first of him,
Monastic ivy say,
Who loves like thee the cloister dim,
And mould'ring turret gray ? —

Lo where with intellectual eye,
In contemplation deep,
He gazes on the starry sky,
Through hours when others sleep.
A graceful form sits by his side,
Among whose ebon curls,
Th' unbidden tears too frequent glide
From her dark eye like pearls.
Too many tears that grief hath cost,
Yet, mother of the dead,
Thou mourn'st the parted, not the lost ·
Then raise thy drooping head.

Woodbine ! sweet woodbine ! softly breathe,
Last, though not loved the less —

Of him who, wild as thy own wreath,
Has all its artlessness?
 The stag, the steed, the mountain wind,
 The birds that sportive skim,
 All joyful things, may to thy mind,
 Present the thought of him!
I ask no more, delightful flowers!
For ye to me have given
Sweet thoughts, and many happy hours
Of thankfulness to Heaven.

———

THE REMONSTRANCE OF THE TRANSPLANTED FLOWERS.

EMMA. C. EMBURY.

Nay, hold, sweet lady, thy cruel hand,
Oh, sever not thus our kindred band,
And look not upon us with pitiless eye,
As on flow'rets born but to blossom and die.

Together we drank the morning dew,
And basked in the glances the sunbeams threw,
And together our sweets we were wont to fling
When zephyr swept by on his radiant wing.

When the purple shadows of evening fell,
'T was sweet to murmur our low farewell

And together, with fragrant sigh to close
Our perfumed blossoms in calm repose.

But now, with none to respond our sigh,
In a foreign home we must droop and die;
The bonds of kindred we once have known,
And how can we live in the world alone?

Ah, lady, list to the voice of mirth,
By childhood wakened around thy hearth,
And think how lonely thy heart would pine,
Should fortune the ties of affection untwine.

E'en now, in the midst of that circle blest,
There are mournful thoughts in thine aching breast,
And how wouldst thou weep, if, bereft of all,
Thou shouldst sit alone in thy empty hall!

———

THE CONSUMPTIVE.

MRS. EMMA C. EMBURY.

The intense desire for fruits and flowers which is generally expressed by the victims of consumption, long after every other taste has
departed, was exemplified in the case of a friend who died while
holding in his hand a tulip.

BRING flowers — fresh flowers — the fairest spring can
        yield,
The poetry of earth, o'er every field,

Scattered in rich display ;
Bring flowers — fresh flowers — around my dying bed,
The sweetness of tne sunny south to shed,
    Ere I am called away.

Bring flowers — fresh flowers — from every sheltered
    glade,
I know their brilliant beauties soon will fade
    Beneath my feverish breath ;
But their bright hues seem to my wandering thought,
With promises of bliss and beauty fraught,
    Winning my heart from death.

Bring flowers — fresh flowers — ere they again shall
    bloom,
I shall be lying in the silent tomb,
    Mouldering in cold decay ;
Bring flowers — fresh flowers — that I may cheer my
    heart
With pleasant images, ere I depart
    To tread the grave's dark way.

Bring fruits — rich fruits — that blush on every bough
Bending above the traveller's weary brow,
    And wooing him to taste ;
Bring fruits — methinks I never knew how sweet
The joys that every day our senses greet,
    Till now in life's swift waste

Bring fruits — rich fruits — earth's fairest gifts are vain
To minister relief to the dull pain
    That steals upon my heart;
Yet bring me fruits and flowers — they still have
    power
To charm if not prolong life's little hour —
    Bring flowers ere I depart.

TO AN AUTUMN ROSE.

CHARLES F. HOFFMAN.

TELL her I love her — love her for those eyes
  Now soft with feeling, radiant now with mirth
Which, like a lake reflecting autumn skies,
  Reveal two heavens here to us on Earth —
The one in which their soulful beauty lies,
  And that wherein such soulfulness has birth.
Go to my lady ere the season flies,
  And the rude winter comes thy bloom to blast —
Go! and with all of Eloquence thou hast,
The burning story of my love discover,
And if the theme should fail, alas! to move her,
Tell her when youth's gay summer-flowers are past
Like thee, my love, will blossom till the last!

INVITATION TO FLOWERS.

BARTON.

Come forth, ye lovely heralds of the Spring!
  Leave, at your Maker's call, your earthly bed;
At his behest your grateful tribute bring
  To light and life, from darkness and the dead!
Thou, timid *Snow-drop*, lift thy lowly head;
  Crocus and *Primrose*, show your varied dye;
Violets, your ceaseless odours round you shed,
  Yourselves the while retiring from the eye,
Yet loading with your sweets each breeze that passes by

And you, — in gay variety, that grace,
  In later months, with beauty the parterre,
'Making a sunshine in the shady place,"
  As Una and her milk-white Lamb were there;
Arise! Arise! and in your turns declare
  The power of Him who has not only made
The depth of Ocean, and the heights of Air,
And Earth's magnificence, — but has display'd
In you that power and skill, with beauty's charms array'd

Uplift, proud *Sun-flower*, to thy favourite Orb
  That disk whereon his brightness loves to dwell;
And, as thou seem'st his radiance to absorb,
  Proclaim thyself The Garden's Sentinel; —
And thou, too, gentle, modest *Heather-bell*,
  Gladden thy lonely birth-place: — *Jasmines*, spread
Your star-like blossoms, fragrant to the smell; —

Yon *Evening Primroses*, when day has fled,
Open your pallid flowers, by dews and moonlight fed.

And where my favourite Abbey* rears on high
Its crumbling ruins, on their loftiest crest
Ye *Wall-flowers*, shed your tints of golden dye,
　　On which the morning sunbeams love to rest,—
On which, when glory fills the glowing west,
　　The parting splendours of the day's decline,
With fascination to the heart address'd,
　　So tenderly and beautifully shine,
As if reluctant still to leave that hoary shrine.

Convolvulus,—expand thy cup-like flower,
　　Graceful in form, and beautiful in hue;—
Clematis, wreathe afresh thy Garden bower,
　　Ye loftier *Lilies*, bathed in morning's dew,
Of purity and innocence renew
　　Each lovely thought;—and ye, whose lowlier pride
In sweet seclusion seems to shrink from view,—
　　You of *The Valley* named, no longer hide
Your blossoms meet to twine the brow of purest Bride.

And Thou, so rich in gentle names, appealing
　　To hearts that own our Nature's common lot;
Thou styled by sportive Fancy's better feeling
　　"*A Thought*,'—" *The Heart's Ease*," or " *Forget me
　　not*,"

---

* Leiston Abbey, in Suffolk.

Who æck'st alike the Peasant's garden-plot,
   An i Castle's proud parterre; — with humble joy
Proclaim afresh, by castle and by cot,
   Hopes which ought not, like things cf time, to cloy,
And feelings Time itself shall deepen — not destroy!

Fruitless, and endless were the task, I ween,
   With ev'ry Flower to grace my votive Lay;
And unto thee, their long-acknowledged QUEEN,
   Fairest, and loveliest! and thy gentle sway,
Beautiful *Rose*, my homage I must pay,—
   For how can Minstrel leave thy charms unsung,
Vhose meek supremacy has been alway
   Confess'd in many a clime, and many a tongue,
And in whose praise the harp of many a Bard has rung ?

Mine is unworthy such a lovely theme; —
   Yet, could I borrow of that tuneful Bird *
Who sings thy praises by the moon's pale beam,
   As Fancy's graceful legends have averr'd,
Those thrilling harmonies at midnight heard,
   With sounds of flowing waters, — not in vain
Should the loose strings of my rude harp be stirr'd
   By inspiration's breath, but one brief strain
Should re-assert thy rites, and celebrate thy reign.

Vain were the hope to rival Bards — whose lyres,
   On such a theme, have left me nought to sing ;-
And one more Plant my humbler Muse inspires,
   Round which my parting thoughts would fondly cling;

---

* The Nightingale.

Which, consecrate to Salem's peaceful King,
　　Though fair as any gracing Beauty's bower,
Is link'd to Sorrow like a holy thing,
　　And takes its Name from Suff'ring's fiercest hour,—
Be this thy noblest fame! imperial PASSION-FLOWER!

Whatever impulse first conferr'd that name,
　　(Or Fancy's dream, or Superstition's art,)
I freely own its spirit-touching claim,
　　With thoughts and feelings it may well impart:—
Not that I would forego the surer chart
　　Of REVELATION — for a mere conceit;
Yet with indulgence may *the Christiar.'s* heart
　　Each frail memorial of HIS MASTER greet,
And chiefly what recalls his Love's most glorious feat.

Be this the closing tribute of my Strain!
　　Be this, *Fair Flowers!* of charms—your last, and best
That when THE SON OF GOD for Man was sla'n,
　　Circled by You, He sank awhile to rest,—
Not *The Grave's* captive, but *A Garden's* guest.
　　So pure and lovely was his transient tomb!
And He, whose brow the *Wreath of Thorns* had press.
　　Not only bore for us Death's cruel doom,
But won *the thornless Crown* of amaranthine blow

BEAUTY AND FRAGRANCE OF FLOWERS.

THOMSON.

BUT, who can paint
Like nature? — Can imagination boast,
Amid its gay creation, hues like hers?
Or can it mix them with that matchless skill,
And lose them in each other, as appears
In ev'ry bud that blows?
Along these blushing borders, bright with dew,
And in yon mingled wilderness of flowers,
Fair-handed Spring unbosoms every grace:
Throws out the snow-drop and the crocus first;
The daisy, primrose, violet, darkly blue,
And polyanthus of unnumber'd dyes;
The yellow wall-flower, stain'd with iron brown,
And lavish stock, that scents the garden round:
From the soft wing of vernal breezes shed,
Anemones, auriculas, enrich'd
With shining meal o'er all their velvet leaves;
And full ranunculus of glowing red.
Then comes the tulip race, where beauty plays
Her idle freaks, from family diffused
To family, as flies the father-dust,
The varied colours run, and while they break
On the charm'd eye, the exulting florist marks,
With secret pride, the wonders of his hand.
No gradual bloom is wanting, from the bud
First-born of spring, to summer's musky tribes;

4

Nor hyacinths, of purest virgin white,
Low-bent, and blushing inward; nor jonquils
Of potent fragrance; nor Narcissus fair,
As o'er the fabled fountain hanging still;
Nor broad carnations, nor gay spotted pinks
Nor, shower'd from ev'ry bush, the damask rose;
Infinite numbers, delicacies, smells,
With hues on hues expression cannot paint,
The breath of nature and her endless bloom.

GARDEN LECTURE.

EVANS.

AMID my garden's broider'd paths I trod,
    And there my mind soon caught her favourite clue,
I seem'd to stand amid the church of God,
    And flowers were preachers, and (still stranger) drew
        From their own life and course
        The love they would enforce,
And sound their doctrine was, and every precept true.

And first the Sunflower spake. Behold, he said,
    How I unweariedly from dawn to night
Turn to the wheeling sun my golden head,
    And drink into my disk fresh draughts of light,
        O mortal! look and learn;
        So, with obedient turn,
From womb to grave pursue the Sun of life and might

And next I heard the lowly Camomile,
　Who, as I trod on him with reckless feet,
And wrang his perfume out, cried, List awhile —
　E'en thus with charity the proud one greet.
　　And, as insulters press,
　　E'en turn thou thus and bless,
And yield from each heart's bruise a redolence more sweet

Then from his rocky pulpit I heard cry
　The Stonecrop. See how loose to earth I grow,
And draw my juicy nurture from the sky.
　So drive not thou, fond man, thy root too low;
　　But, loosely clinging here,
　　From God's supernal sphere
Draw life's unearthly food, catch heaven's undying glow

Then preach'd the humble Strawberry. Behold
　The lowliest and least adorn'd of flowers
Lies at thy feet; yet lift my leafy fold,
　And fruit is there unfound in gaudier bowers.
　　So plain be thou, and meek,
　　And when vain man shall seek,
Unveil the blooming fruit of solitary hours.

Then cried the Lily: Hear my mission next.
　On me thy Lord bade ponder and be wise,
Oh! wan with toil, with care and doubt perplext,
　Survey my joyous bloom, my radiant dyes.
　　My hues no vigils dim,
　　All care I cast on Him
Who more than faith can ask each hour to faith supplies

The Thistle warn'd me last; for, as I tore
    The intruder up, it cried, Rash man, take heed!
In me thou hast thy type.   Yea, pause and pore—
    Even as thou, doth God his vineyard weed;
       Deem not each worthier plant
       For thee shall waste and want,
Nor fright with hostile spines thy Master's chosen seed

Then cried the garden's host with one consent:
    Come, man, and see how, day by day, we shoot
For every hour of rain, and sunshine lent,
    Deepen our glowing hues, and drive our root;
       And, as our heads we lift,
       Record each added gift,
And bear to God's high will, and man's support, our fruit

O Leader thou of earth's exulting quire,
    Thou with a first-born's royal rights endued,
Wilt thou alone be dumb? alone desire
    Renew'd the gifts so oft in vain renew'd?
       Then sicken, fret, and pine,
       As on thy head they shine,
And wither 'mid the bliss of boundless plenitude?

Oh, come! and, as thy due, our concert lead.
    Glory to him, the Lord of life and light,
Who nursed our tender leaf, our colours spread,
    And gave thy body mind, the first-born's right,
       By which thy flight may cleave
       The starry pole, and leave
Thy younger mates below in death's unbroken night

GARDEN THOUGHTS.

MONTGOMERY.

Written on occasion of a Ladies' Bazaar, in aid of the Church Missionary Society, being held in the garden-grounds of a benevolent family resident on the banks of the Yorkshire Ouse.

In a garden — Man was placed,
Meet abode for innocence ;
With his Maker's image graced :
Sin crept in, and drove him thence,
Through the world, a wretch undone,
Seeking rest and finding none.

In a garden, — On that night
When our Saviour was betray'd,
With what world-redeeming might,
In his agony he pray'd !
Till he drank the vengeance up,
And with mercy fill'd the cup.

In a garden, — on the cross,
When the spear his heart had riven,
And for earth's primeval loss
Heaven's own ransom had been given,
Jesus rested from his woes,
Jesus from the dead arose.

Here, not Eden's bowers are found,
Nor the lone Gethsemane,
Nor the calm sepulchral ground
At the foot of Calvary :
4*

But th's scene may well recal.
Sweet remembrances of all.

Emblem of the church below!
Where the Spirit and the Word
Fall like dew, like breezes blow;
And the Lord God's voice is heard,
Walking in the cool of day,
When the world is far away:

Emblem of the church above,
Where, amidst their native clime,
In the garden of his love,
Rescued from the storms of time,
Saints, as trees of life, shall stand,
Planted by the Lord's right hand:

Round the fair enclosure here,
Flames no cherub's threatening sword;
Ye who enter! feel no fear:
Roof'd by heaven, with verdure floor'd,
Breathing balm from blossoms gay,
This be Paradise to-day!

Yet one moment meditate
On that dreary banishment,
When from Eden's closing gate,
Hand in hand, our parents went;
Spikenard-groves no more to dress,
But a thorny wilderness.

Then remember Him, who laid
Uncreated splendour by;
Lower than the angels made,
Fallen man to glorify,
And from death beyond the grave,
An apostate world to save.

Think of Him · your souls He sought,
Wandering never to return.
Hath he found you?—At the thought
All your hearts within you burn.
Then your love like His extend;
Be, like Him, the sinner's friend.

O'er the city Jesus wept,
Doom'd to perish:—Won't *you* weep
O'er a world, by Satan kept,
Dreaming in delirious sleep,
'Till the twinkle of an eye
Wakes them in eternity?

Ye, who smile with rosy youth,
Glow in manhood, fade through years,
Send the life, the light, the truth,
To dead hearts, blind eyes, deaf ears;
And your very pleasure make
Charities, for Jesus' sake.

So shall gospel-glory run
Round the globe, through every clime,
Brighter than the circling sun;
Hastening that millennial time

When the earth shall be restored,
As the garden of the Lord.

Ye, who own this quiet place,
Here, like Enoch, walk with God;
And, till summon'd hence, through grace,   ⁰
Tread the path your Saviour trod,
Then to Paradise on high,
With the wings of angels fly

COLLECTION OF FLOWERS.

ILLUSTRATION OF THE PLATE

Fringed Pink.

Disdain.

Away! I seek no smile of thine;
  Within those shining eyes,
The trifler's soul, revealed to mine,
  Doth wear no vain disguise.

Thy words are weighed with costly art,
  They come not wil lly free —
Oh! never hath my spirit part
  With one I deem like thee.

                                L. H

LANGUAGE OF FLOWERS.

CHARLES F. HOFFMAN.

TEACH thee their language? sweet, I know no tongue,
    No mystic art those gentle things declare,
I ne'er could trace the schoolman's trick among
    Created things, so delicate and rare
Their language. Prythee! why they are themselves
    But bright thoughts syllabled to shape and hue,
The tongue that erst was spoken by the elves,
    When tenderness as yet within the world was new

And still how oft their soft and starry eyes—
    Now bent to earth, to heaven now mutely pleading
Their incense fainting as it seeks the skies,
    Yet still from earth with freshening hope receding-
How often these to every heart declare,
    With all the silent eloquence of truth,
The language that they speak is Nature's prayer,
    To give her back those spotless days of youth.

THE SNOW-DROP.

THE Snow-drop (which may be found in meadows and orchards) receives its name from the whiteness of its flower, and the time of its appearance, which is often when snow is on the ground. Its botanical appellation is *Galanthus nivalis,* or snowy milk flower.

The Snow-drop, considered as the harbinger of spring and the promise of future blessings, is the most cheering and welcome of plants. Rearing its spotless head amid frost and storm, it gives joyous sign of that coming season which is to restore the delights of budding flowers and sunny skies. But there are some persons who, though "skilled in nature's lore," deny that it is adapted to awaken pleasing anticipations. "The Snow-drop," writes Mr. Knapp,* "is a melancholy flower. The season in which the 'Fair maids of February' come out, is the most dreary and desolate of our year: they peep through the snow that often surrounds them, shivering and cheerless; they convey no idea of reviving nature, and are scarcely the harbingers of milder days, but rather the emblem of sleety storms, and icy gales, (snow-drop weather,) and wrap their petals round the infant germ, fearing to admit the very air that blows; and when found beyond the verge of cultivation, they most generally remind us of some

---

* See "Journal of a Naturalist."

deserted dwelling, a family gone, a hearth that smokes
no more."

———

ALREADY now the snow-drop dares appear.
The first pale blossom of th' unripen'd year:
As Flora's breath, by some transforming power,
Had changed an icicle into a flower.
Its name and hue the scentless plant retains,
And winter lingers in its icy veins.

BARBAULD.

OH! sweetly beautiful it is to mark
    The virgin, vernal snow-drop! lifting up —
    Meek as a nun — the whiteness of its cup,
From earth's dead bosom, desolate and dark.

ANON.

FIRST in bright Flora's train Galantha glows,
And prints with frolic step the melting snows:
Chides with her dulcet voice the tardy spring,
Bids slumbering Zephyr stretch his folded wing,
Wakes the hoarse cuckoo in his gloomy cave,
And calls the wandering dormouse from his grave
Bids the mute redbreast cheer the budding grove,
And plaintive ringdove tune her notes to love.

DARWIN.

THE SNOW-DROP.

SMITH.

LIKE pendent flakes of vegetating snow,
The early herald of the infant year,
Ere yet the adventurous crocus dares to blow,
Beneath the orchard boughs thy buds appear.

While still the cold north-east ungenial lowers,
And scarce the hazel in the leafless copse
Or sallows show their downy powder'd flowers,
The grass is spangled with thy silver drops.

Yet when those pallid blossoms shall give place
To countless tribes of richer hue and scent,—
Summer's gay blooms, and Autumn's yellow race,
I shall thy pale inodorous bells lament.

So journeying onward in life's varying track,
E'en while warm youth its bright illusion lends,
Fond memory often with regret looks back
To childhood's pleasure and to infant friends.

The same. — LANGHORNE.

POETS still, in graceful numbers,
    May the glowing roses choose;
But the Snow-drop's simple beauty
    Better suits an humble Muse.

5*

Earliest bud that decks the garden,
  Fairest of the fragrant race,
First-born child of vernal Flora,
  Seeking mild thy lowly place;

Though no warm or murmuring zephyr
  Fan thy leaves with balmy wing,
Pleased we hail thee, spotless blossom,
  Herald of the infant Spring.

Through the cold and cheerless season
  Soft thy tender form expands,
Safe in unaspiring graces,
  Foremost of the bloomy bands.

White-robed flower, in lonely beauty
  Rising from a wintry bed;
Chilling winds, and blasts ungenial,
  Rudely threat'ning round thy head.

Silvery bud, thy pensile foliage
  Seems the angry blasts to fear;
Yet secure, thy tender texture
  Ornaments the rising year.

No warm tints, or vivid col'ring,
  Paint thy bells with gaudy pride,
Mildly charm'd, we seek thy fragrance,
  Where no thorns insidious hide

'Tis not thine, with flaunting beauty
  To attract the roving sight;
Nature, from her varied wardrobe,
  Chose thy vest of purest white.

White, as falls the fleecy shower,
  Thy soft form in sweetness grows;
Not more fair the valley's treasure,
  Not more sweet her lily blows.

Drooping harbinger of Flora,
  Simply are thy blossoms drest;
Artless as the gentle virtues,
  Mansion'd in the blameless breast.

When to pure and timid virtue   .
  Friendship twines a votive wreath,
O'er the fair selected garden
  Thou thy perfume soft shalt breathe.

The same. — MONTGOMERY.

WINTER, retire!
Thy reign is past;
Hoary Sire!
Yield the sceptre of thy sway,
Sound thy trumpet in the blast,
And call thy storms away:
Winter, retire!
Wherefore do thy wheels delay
Mount the chariot of thine ire,
And quit the realms of day;

On thy state
Whirlwinds wait·
And blood-shot meteors lend thee light,
Hence to dreary arctic regions,
Summon thy terrific legions;
Hence to caves of northern night
Speed thy flight.

From halcyon seas
And purer skies,
O southern breeze'
Awake, arise:
Breath of heaven! benignly blow,
Melt the snow;
Breath of heaven! unchain the floods,
Warm the woods,
And make the mountains flow.

Auspicious to the Muse's prayer,
The freshening gale
Embalms the vale,
And breathes enchantment through the airs
On its wing
Floats the spring
With glowing eye, and golden hair·
Dark before her angel-form,
She drives the Demon of the storm,
Like Gladness chasing Care.

Winter's gloomy night withdrawn,
Lo! the young romantic Hours

Search the hill, the dale, the lawn,
To behold the SNOW-DROP white
Start to light,
And shine in Flora's desert bowers,
Beneath the vernal dawn,
The Morning Star of Flowers!

O welcome to our isle,
Thou Messenger of peace!
At whose bewitching smile
The embattled tempests cease;
Emblem of Innocence and Truth!
First-born of Nature's womb,
When strong in renovated youth,
She bursts from Winter's tomb;
Thy parent's eye hath shed
A precious dew-drop on thine head,
Frail as a mother's tear
Upon her infant's face,
When ardent hope to tender fear,
And anxious love, gives place.
But lo! the dew-drop flits away,
The sun salutes thee with a ray
Warm as a mother's kiss,
Upon her infant's cheek,
When the heart bounds with bliss,
And joy that cannot speak!
—When I meet thee by the way,
Like a pretty, sportive child,
On the winter-wasted wild.

With thy darling breeze at play,
Opening to the radiant sky
All the sweetness of thine eye;
—Or bright with sunbeams, fresh with showers,
O thou Fairy-Queen of flowers!
Watch thee o'er the plain advance
At the head of Flora's dance;
Simple SNOW-DROP! then in thee
All thy sister-train I see:
Every brilliant bud that blows,
From the blue-bell to the rose;
All the beauties that appear
On the bosom of the year;
All that wreathe the locks of Spring,
Summer's ardent breath perfume,
Or on the lap of Autumn bloom,
All to thee their tribute bring,
Exhale their incense at thy shrine,
—Their hues, their odours all are thine!
For while thy humble form I view,
The Muse's keen prophetic sight
Brings fair Futurity to light,
And Fancy's magic makes the vision true.

—There is a Winter in my soul,
The Winter of despair;
Oh! when shall Spring its rage control?
When shall the SNOW-DROP blossom there?
Cold gleams of comfort sometimes dart
A dawn of glory on my heart

But quickly pass away :
Thus Northern lights the gloom adorn,
And give the promise of a morn
That never turns to day !
— But hark ! methinks I hear
A small still whisper in mine ear ;
" Rash youth, repent !
" Afflictions, from above,
" Are Angels sent
" On embassies of love.
" A fiery legion, at thy birth,
" Of chastening woes were given,
" To pluck thy flowers of Hope from earth,
" And plant them high
" O'er yonder sky,
" Transform'd to stars, — and fix'd in heaven."

The same. — HOWITT.

THE Snow-drop ! 'tis an English flower,
And grows beneath our garden trees :
For every heart it has a dower
Of old and dear remembrances ;
All look upon it, and straightway
Recall their youth, like yesterday ! —
Their sunny years, when forth they went
Wandering in weariless content ;
Their little plot of garden ground,
The pleasant orchard's quiet bound ;

Their father's home, so free from care,
And the familiar faces there:

The household voices, kind and sweet,
That knew no feigning — hush'd and gone!
The mother that was sure to greet
Their coming with a welcome tone;
The brothers, that were children then.
Now anxious, thoughtful, toiling men;
And the kind sisters, whose glad mirth
Was like a sunshine on the earth;—
These come back to the heart supine,
Flower of our youth! at look of thine;
And thou, among the dimm'd and gone,
Art an unalter'd thing alone!

Unchanged, unchanged the very flower
That grew in Eden droopingly,
Which now, beside the peasant's door
Awakes his merry children's glee,
E'en as it fill'd his heart with joy,
Beside his mother's door — a boy:
The same, and to his heart it brings
The freshness of those vanish'd springs.
Bloom, then, fair flower! in sun and shade
For deep thought in thy cup is laid,
And careless children, in their glee,
A sacred memory make of thee.

THE SNOW-DROP'S CALL.

MISS E. EMRA.

Who else is coming?—There's sunshine here!
Ye would strew the way for the infant year:
The frost-winds blow on the barren hill,
And icicles hang on the quarry still;
But sunny, and shelter'd, and safe, are we,
In the moss at the foot of the sycamore tree.

Are ye not coming? the first birds sing;
They call to her bowers the lingering Spring;
And, afar to his home near the north-pole star
Old Winter is gone in his snow-clad car;
And the storms are past, and the sky is clear,
And we are alone, sweet sisters! here.

Will ye not follow? Ye safe shall be
In the green moss under the sycamore tree.
And, oh! there is health in the clear cold breeze,
And a sound of joy in the leafless trees;
And the sun is pale, yet his pleasant gleam
Has waken'd the earth, and unchain'd the stream
And the soft west-wind, oh, it gently blows!
Hasten to follow, pale lady Primrose!
And Hyacinth graceful, and Crocus gay,
For we have not met this many a day.
Follow us, follow us! follow us then,
All ye whose home is in grove or glen.
Why do ye linger? Who else is coming,
Now Spring is awake with the wild bees' humming?

6

THE PRIMROSE

The botanic name, Primula, is derived from *primus*, first, *prime*, or early, and hence prime-*rose* contracted into primrose.

This little flower, in itself so fair, shows yet fairer from he early season of its appearance; peeping forth even from the retreating snows of winter. It forms a happy shade of union between the delicate Snow-drop and the flaming Cro-cus, which also venture forth in the very dawn of spring.

————

Bring the rathe primrose that forsaken dies.

LYCIDAS.

————Pale primroses
That die unmarried, ere they can behold
Bright Phœbus in his strength.

WINTER'S TALE.

The yellow cowslip and the pale primrose.

MILTON'S MAY MORNING.

Oh! who can speak his joys when spring's young morn
From wood and pasture open'd on his view,
When tender green buds blush upon the thorn,
And the first primrose dips its leaves in dew!

And while he pluck'd the primrose in its pride,
He ponder'd o'er its bloom, 'tween joy and pain;
And a rude sonnet in its praise he tried,
Where nature's simple way the aid of art supplied.

CLARE.
(60)

TO THE PRIMROSE.

ANON.

MARK in yonder thorny vale,
　Fearless of the falling snows,
Careless of the chilly gale,
　Passing sweet the *Primrose* blows.

Milder gales and warmer beams
　May the gaudier flow'rets rear;
But to me the Primrose seems
　Proudest gem that decks the year.

THE EARLY PRIMROSE

H. K. WHITE.

MILD offspring of a dark and sullen sire!
Whose modest form, so delicately fine,
　Was nursed in whirling storms,
　And cradled in the winds.

Thee, when young Spring first question'd Winter's sway,
And dared the sturdy blusterer to the fight,
　Thee on this bank he threw,
　To mark his victory.

In this low vale, the promise of the year,
Serene, thou openest to the nipping gale,
　Unnoticed and alone,
　Thy tender elegance.

So Virtue blooms, brought forth amid the storms
Of chill adversity; in some lone walk
    Of life she rears her head,
    Obscure and unobserved; —

While every bleaching breeze tha. on her brows.
Chastens her spotless purity of breast,
    And hardens her to bear,
    Serene, the ills of life.

THE PRIMROSE.

MRS. HEMANS.

I SAW it in my evening walk,
    A little lonely flower;
Under a hollow bank it grew,
    Deep in a mossy bower.

An oak's gnarl'd root to roof the cave,
    With gothic fretwork sprung,
Whence jewell'd fern, and arum leaves,
    And ivy garlands hung.

And close beneath came sparkling out,
    From an old tree's fallen shell,
A little rill, that clipt about
    The lady in her cell.

And there, methought, with bashful pride
    She seem'd to sit and look
On her own maiden loveliness,
    Pale imaged in the brook.

No other flower, no rival grew
    Beside my pensive maid;
She dwelt alone, a cloister'd nun
    In solitude and shade.

No sunbeam on that fairy pool,
    Darted its dazzling light;
Only, methought, some clear, cold star
    Might tremble there at night.

No ruffling wind could reach her there,
    No eye, methought, but mine;
Or the young lambs that came to drink,
    Had spied her secret shrine.

And there was pleasantness to me
    In such belief; — cold eyes
That slight dear Nature's loveliness,
    Profane her mysteries.

Long time I look'd and linger'd there,
    Absorb'd in still delight;
My spirit drank deep quietness
    In, with that quiet sight.

The same. — CLARE.

WELCOME, pale Primrose! starting up between
    Dead matted leaves of ash and oak, that strew
    The very lawn, the wood, and spinney through,
'Mid creeping moss and ivy's darker green:

How much thy presence beautifies the ground!
How sweet thy modest, unaffected pride
Glows on the sunny bank, and wood's warm side.

    And where thy fairy flowers in groups are found,
The school-boy roams enchantedly along,
    Plucking the fairest with a rude delight:
While the meek shepherd stops his simple song,

    To gaze a moment on the pleasing sight;
O'erjoy'd to see the flowers that truly bring
The welcome news of sweet returning Spring.

The Same. — MICKLE.

SAY, gentle lady of the bower,
    For thou, though young, art wise;
And known to thee is every flower
    Beneath our milder skies:

Say, which the plant of modest dye,
    And lovely mien combined,
That fittest to the pensive eye
    Displays the virtuous mind.

I sought the garden's boasted haunt;
    But on the gay parterre
Carnations glow, and tulips flaunt, —
    No humble flow'ret there.

The flower you seek, the nymph replies,
  Has bow'd the languid head;   .
For on its bloom the blazing skies
  Their sultry rage have shed.

Yet search yon shade obscure, forlorn,
  Where rude the bramble grows;
There, shaded by the humble thorn,
  The lingering primrose blows.

TO PRIMROSES FILLED WITH MORNING DEW.

HERRICK.

Why do you weep? Can tears
    Speak grief in you
    Who were but born
  Just as the modest morn
  Teem'd her refreshing dew?

Alas! you have not known that shower
    That mars a flower;
    Nor felt th' unkind
  Breath of a blasting wind;
  Nor are ye worn with years;
    Nor warp'd as we,
  Who think it strange to see
Such pretty flowers, like to orphans young,
To speak by tears before ye have a tongue.

Speak, * * * * and make known
      The reason why
      Ye droop and weep.
   Is it for want of sleep,
  Or childish lullaby?
Or that ye have not seen as yet
      The violet?

     *   *   *   *   *

     *   *   *   *   *

  No, no; this sorrow, shown
    By your tears shed,
  Would have this lecture read,
That things of greatest, so of meaner sort,
   Conceived with grief are, and with tears brought forth

COWSLIP.

The name of Cowslip seems to be derived from the Saxon   Cuslippe, and was probably given to the flower on account of the resemblance which its perfume has to the breath of a cow, or from its being so closely pressed by the lip of the cow in the pastures, where it is considered an injurious weed.

The Primrose seeks the partial shade of hedgerows, the banks of sheltered lanes, and the borders of woods and coppices, delighting in concealment; but the Cowslip advances boldly into the open fields, and decorates the sloping hills with its pendent umbels of fragrant blossoms.

The corollas of the Cowslip are often gathered to make a kind of liqueur wine, which is thought to promote sleep

> " Thy little sons
> Permit to range the pastures; gladly they
> Will mow the Cowslip posies, faintly sweet,
> From whence thou artificial wines shalt drain
> Of icy taste, that, in mid fervours, best
> Slack craving thirst, and mitigate the day."
>
> PHILLIPS.

How cheerful along the gay mead,
The Daisy and Cowslip appear!

When April's smiles the flowery lawn adorn,
  And modest Cowslips deck the streamlet's side;
When fragrant orchards to the roseate morn
  Unfold their bloom, in heaven's own colours dyed.

The flowery May, who from her green lap throws
The yellow Cowslip and the pale Primrose.

MILTON

Where the bee sucks, there lurk I;
In a Cowslip's bell I lie:
There I couch when owls do cry.

TEMPEST.

Whilst from off the waters fleet
Thus I set my printless feet
O'er the Cowslip's velvet head
That bends not as I tread.

MILTON

———— rich in vegetable gold,
From calyx pale the freckled Cowslip born,
Receives in amber cup the fragrant dews of morn.

ANON.

—— Cowslips wan, that hang the pensive head.

MILTON

COWSLIP.

ON FINDING AN EARLY COWSLIP.

ANON.

It is the same! It is the very scent —
That bland, yet luscious, meadow-breathing sweet
Which I remember when my childish feet,
With new life's rejoicing spirit, went
Through the deep grass with wild flow'rs richly blent,
That smiled to high Heav'n from their verdant seat,
But it brings not to thee such joy complete:
Thou canst not see, as I do, how we spent
In blessedness, in sunshine, and in flowers,
The beautiful noon; and then, how, seated round
The odorous pile, upon the shaded ground,
A boyish group — we laugh'd away the hours,
Plucking the yellow blooms for future wine,
While o'er us play'd a mother's smile divine.

———

COWSLIPS.

HOWITT.

Oh! fragrant dwellers of the lea,
  When first the wild wood rings
With each sound of vernal minstrelsy
  When fresh the green grass springs.

What can the blessed Spring restore
  More gladdening than your charms
Bringing the memory once more
  Of lovely fields and farms!

Of thickets, breezes, birds, and flowers;
Of life's unfolding prime;
Of thoughts as cloudless as the hours;
Of souls without a crime.

Oh! blessed, blessed do ye seem,
For, even now, I turn'd,
With soul athirst for wood and stream,
From streets that glared and burn'd:

From the hot town, where mortal care
His crowded fold doth pen;
Where stagnates the polluted air
In many a sultry den.

And ye are here! and ye are here!
Drinking the dewlike wine,
'Midst living gales, and waters clear,
And heaven's unstinted shine.

I care not that your little life
Will quickly have run through,
And the sward, with summer children rife
Keep not a trace of you.

For again, again, on dewy plain,
I trust to see you rise,
When spring renews the wild wood strain,
And bluer gleam the skies.

Again, again, when many springs
Upon my grave shall shine,
Here shall you speak of vanish'd things,
To living hearts of mine.

THE DAISY

WE presume that this flower was called daisy or day's-eye, from the nature of its blossom, which expands at the opening of day and closes at sunset.

> The little dazie that at evening closes.
> SPENSER.

> By a daisy, whose leaves spread,
> Shut when Titan goes to bed.
> G. WITHERS.

The most careless observer of plants must have noticed, that the daisy not only closes its petals at night, but that they are also carefully folded over the yellow disk in rainy weather. It must likewise have struck the attention of the curious, that not only this flower, but most others which are natives of moist climates, have the power, we may almost say instinct, of securing their essential parts of fructification from the rains of the day or the dews of the night, whilst those of regular dry climates are quite destitute of this wise provision of nature.

> BY dimpled brook and fountain brim,
> The wood-nymphs, deck'd with daisies trim,
> Their merry wakes and pastimes keep.
> MILTON'S COMUS

> —— in the spring and play-time of the year,
> That calls the unwonted villager abroad
> With all her little ones, a sportive train,

To ga.her kingcups in the yellow mead,
And prank their hair with daisies.

COWPER.

THE daisy scatter'd on each mead and down,
A golden tuft within a silver crown;
Fair fall that dainty flower! and may there be
No shepherd graced that doth not honour thee!

W. BROWNE.

FOR scarcely on Devonia's genial sky
The faithful daisy shuts her watchful eye!

CARRINGTON.

TO A DAISY, BLOOMING IN THE DEPTH OF WINTER

MILLHOUSE.

Too forward Beauty! was it wisely done,
   Thus premature to throw thy virgin charms
   Into decrepit January's arms?
A tardy wooer he; for, lo! his sun
   With grudging aspect gives a feeble ray.
Soon will the circle of thy joys be run;
Thy spring shall finish ere 'tis well begun,
   Nor ever greet the nuptial tribes of May.
   E'en while thou dost unfold thy bosom gay,
I hear the tempest muttering in the north;
The breezes, keener-edged, are coming forth;
   And how shalt thou withstand the icy fray?
Sweet floret! while *thy* fate I thus bemoan,
Gloomy anticipation paints my own.

THE DAISY.

ON FINDING ONE IN FULL BLOOM ON CHRISTMAS DAY

MONTGOMERY.

THERE is a flower, a little flower,
With silver crest and golden eye,
That welcomes every changing hour,
And weathers every sky.

The prouder beauties of the field,
In gay but quick succession shine;
Race after race their honours yield —
They flourish and decline.

But this small flower, to Nature dear,
While moons and stars their courses run,
Wreathes the whole circle of the year,
Companion of the sun.

It smiles upon the lap of May,
To sultry August spreads its charms,
Lights pale October on his way,
And twines December's arms.

The purple heath, and golden broom,
On moory mountains catch the gale.
O'er lawns the lily sheds perfume,
The violet in he vale.

But this bold floweret climbs the hill,
Hides in the forest, haunts the glen,
Plays on the margin of the rill,
Peeps round the fox's den.

7*

Within the garden's cultured round
It shares the sweet carnation's bed;
And blooms on consecrated ground,
In honour of the dead.

The lambkin crops its crimson gem;
The wild bee murmurs on its breast;
The blue-fly bends its pensile stem,
Light, o'er the sky-lark's nest.

'T is Flora's page:—In every place,
In every season, fresh and fair,
It opens with perennial grace,
And blossoms everywhere.

On waste and woodland, rock and plain,
Its humble buds unheeded rise:
The rose has but a summer reign;
The daisy never dies.

The same. — LEYDEN.

STAR of the mead! sweet daughter of the day,
Whose opening flower invites the morning ray,
From thy moist cheek, and bosom's chill fold,
To kiss the tears of eve, the dew-drops cold!
Sweet Daisy, flower of love! when birds are pair'd,
'T is sweet to see thee with thy bosom bared,
Smiling, in virgin innocence, serene,
Thy pearly crown above thy vest of green.
The lark, with sparkling eye, and rustling wing,
Rejoins his widow'd mate in early spring,

And as she prunes his plumes, of russet hue,
Swears, on thy maiden blossom, to be true.

Oft have I watch'd thy closing buds at eve,
Which for the parting sun-beams seem'd to grieve,
And, when gay morning gilt the dew-bright plain,
Seen them unclasp their folded leaves again :
Nor he who sung — ' the Daisy is so sweet ' —
More dearly loved thy pearly form to greet ;
When on his scarf the knight the Daisy bound,
And dames at tourneys shone, with daisies crown'd
And fays forsook the purer fields above,
To hail the daisy, flower of faithful love.

The same. — WORDSWORTH.

WITH little here to do or see
Of things that in the great world be,
Sweet Daisy ! oft I talk to thee,
   For thou art worthy, —
Thou unassuming Common-place
Of nature, with that homely face,
And yet with something of a grace,
   Which Love makes for thee !

Oft on the dappled turf at ease
I sit, and play with similies,
Loose types of Things through all degrees,
   Thoughts of thy raising :
And many a fond and idle name
I give to thee, for praise or blame,

As is the humour of the game,
  While I am gazing.

A Nun demure, of lowly port;
Or sprightly Maiden, of Love's Court,
In thy simplicity the sport
  Of all temptations;
A Queen in crown of rubies drest;
A Starveling in a scanty vest;
Are all, as seems to suit thee best,
  Thy appellations.

A little Cyclops, with one eye
Staring to threaten and defy,
That thought comes next—and instant;
  The freak is over,
The shape will vanish, and behold
A silver Shield with boss of gold,
That spreads itself, some Faery bold
  In fight to cover!

I see thee glittering from afar;—
And then thou art a pretty Star;
Not quite so fair as many are
  In heaven above thee!
Yet like a star, with glittering crest,
Self-poised in air thou seem'st to rest,—
May peace come never to his nest,
  Who shall reprove thee!

Sweet Flower! for by that name at last,
When all my reveries are past,
I call thee, and to that cleave fast.
Sweet silent creature!
That breath'st with me in sun and air,
Do thou, as thou art wont, repair
My heart with gladness, and a share
Of thy meek nature!

TO A MOUNTAIN DAISY.

ON TURNING ONE DOWN WITH THE PLOUGH.

BURNS.

Wee, modest, crimson-tipped flower,
Thou'st met me in an evil hour,
For I must crush among the stoure
Thy slender stem:
To spare thee now is past my power,
Thou bonny gem!

Alas! 'tis not thy neighbour sweet,
The bonny lark, companion meet,
Bending thee 'mong the dewy wheat,
With speckled breast —
When upward springing, blithe to greet
The purpling east.

Cold blew the bitter-biting north
Upon thy early humble birth;

Yet cheerfully thou venturest forth
    Amid the storm,
Scarce rear'd above the parent earth
    Thy tender form.

The flaunting flowers our gardens yield,
High-shelt'ring woods and wall must shield;
But thou between the random bield
    Of clod or stone,
Adorn'st the rugged stubble field,
    Unseen, alone.

There, in thy scanty mantle clad,
Thy snowy bosom sunward spread.
Thou lift'st thy unassuming head
    In humble guise:
But now the share uptears thy bed,
    And low it lies!

THE MICHAELMAS DAISY.

ANON.

Last smile of the departing year,
Thy sister-sweets are flown!
Thy pensive wreath is far more dear
From blooming thus alone.

Thy tender blush, thy simple frame,
Unnoticed might have pass'd;
But now thou com'st with softer claim,
The loveliest and the last.

Sweet are the charms in thee we find,—
Emblem of hope's gay wing;
'Tis thine to call past bloom to mind,
To promise future spring.

The same.—MISS MITFORD.

WITHIN my little garden is a flower—
A tuft of flowers, most like a sheaf of corn,
The lilac-blossom'd daisy that is born
At Michaelmas, wrought by the gentle power
Of this sweet Autumn into one bright shower
Of blooming beauty. Spring hath nought more fair—
Four sister butterflies inhabit there:
Gay, gentle creatures! Round that odorous bower
They weave their dance of joy the livelong day,
Seeming to bless the sunshine; and at night
Fold their enamell'd wings, as if to pray.
Home-loving pretty ones! would that I might
For richer gifts as cheerful tribute pay,
So meet the rising dawn, so hail the parting ray.

SWEET VIOLET.

WHAT the origin of the word Viola is, cannot be precisely determined. It has been fabled, however, that the Greek name of the plant, Ιον (ion), is taken from the circumstance, that, when the nymph Io was changed by Jupiter into a cow, this plant sprang from the earth to become her food. From the same fable the term Viola is supposed to have had its origin, *viola* being formed from *vitula* (which means a young cow) by dropping the *t*.

The Viola Odorata, or Sweet Violet, is a native of every part of Europe, in woods, bushes, and hedges, flowering in March and April. The flower varies in colour, though most commonly a deep purple: it is sometimes of a pale purple, sometimes of a red purple, flesh-coloured, or quite white; but it is always delightfully fragrant.

The growth of the Sweet Violet is not confined to Europe; it perfumes the paler groves of Barbary during winter, it flourishes in Palestine, and both Japan and China boast of this fragrant flower. Hasselquist tells us that it is one of the plants most esteemed in Syria, and particularly on account of its great use in sherbet, which is made with violet sugar.

———————

——— LET the beauteous Violet
Be planted, which, with purple and with gold
Richly adorn'd, ———
And that which creeps pale-colour'd on the ground.

COLUMELLA

(84)

————— Violets, dim,
But sweeter than the lids of Juno's eyes,
Or Cytherea's breath.

WINTER'S TALE.

———— the trembling Violet, which eyes
The sun but once, and unrepining dies.

And Violets, whose looks are like the skies.

BARRY CORNWALL.

————— steals timidly away,
Shrinking as Violets do in summer's ray.

That strain again! it had a dying fall:
Oh! it came o'er my ear like the sweet south,
That breathes upon a bank of Violets,
Stealing and giving odour.

TWELFTH NIGHT.

TO AN EARLY VIOLET.

HOWITT.

HERALD of brighter hours! why from thy rest
   Thus early dost thou start? chill is the gale
   To form, like thine, so beautiful and frail.
The rook, with careful cries that seeks its nest,
Flings its broad shadow on thy dewy breast.
   For sunny is the day, though like the smile
   Dear woman wears, when she would fain beguile
   coldness of her fortune. Upward towers

8

The lark, companion of the fields, with thee,
And sings unto the clouds his songs of glee!
Perchance his skyward dreams are of the flow'rs
Which gather round him in June's radiant hours;
When thou, fair comer of the spring, hast shed
Thy perfumed breath abroad, and droop'd upon thy
bed.

The same. — ANON.

SWEET, lovely harbinger of Spring,
Earliest gift in Flora's ring,
Thy scent exhales on Zephyr's wing,
                    Sweet Violet!

I found you in the lone vale bare,
In purest hue, sweet flow'ret rare,
And you shall have my dearest care,
                    Sweet Violet!

You stood like dauntless Virtue pure,
You did the pitiless storm endure,
And now from harm I'll you secure,
                    Sweet Violet

Within my jessamine parterre,
'Mid myrtles sweet, and lilies fair,
You now may live, and blossom there,
                    Sweet Violet!

VIOLETS.—A SONNET.

BARTON.

BEAUTIFUL are you in your lowliness;
  Bright in your hues, delicious in 'your scent;
  Lovely your modest blossoms, downward bent,
As shrinking from our gaze, yet prompt to bless
The passer-by with fragrance, and express
  How gracefully, though mutely eloquent,
  Are unobtrusive worth, and meek content,
Rejoicing in their own obscure recess.
  Delightful flowerets! at the voice of Spring
  Your buds unfolded to its sunbeams bright;
  And though your blossoms soon shall fade from sight,
Above your lowly birth-place birds shall sing,
And from your clust'ring leaves the glow-worm fling
  The emerald glory of its earth-born light.

The same. — SMITH.

SWEET Violets! from your humble beds
Among the moss, beneath the thorn,
You rear your unprotected heads,
And brave the cold and cheerless morn
Of early March; not yet are past
The wintry cloud, the sullen blast,
Which, when your fragrant buds shall blow,
May lay those purple beauties low.
Ah! stay awhile, till warmer showers,
And brighter suns, shall cheer the day!

Sweet Violets stay, till hardier flowers
Prepare to meet the lovely May.
Then from your mossy shelter come,
And rival every richer bloom;
For though their colours gayer shine,
Their odours do not equal thine.
And thus real merit still may dare to vie
With all that wealth bestows, or pageant heraldry

TO A VIOLET.

BOWRING.

SWEET flower! Spring's earliest, loveliest gem
  While other flowers are idly sleeping,
Thou rear'st thy purple diadem,
  Meekly from thy seclusion peeping.

Thou, from thy little secret mound,
  Where diamond dew-drops shine above thee
Scatterest thy modest fragrance round;
  And well may Nature's Poet love thee!

Thine is a short, swift reign, I know;
  But here, thy spirit still pervading,
New Violets' tufts again shall blow,
  Then fade away — as thou art fading —

And be renew'd; the hope how blest,
  (Oh may that hope desert me never!) —
Like thee to sleep on Nature's breast,
  And wake again, and bloom for ever

TO A YELLOW VIOLET

ANON.

WHEN beechen buds begin to swell,
   And woods the blue-birds' warble know,
The yellow Violet's modest bell
   Peeps from the last year's leaves below.

Ere russet fields their green resume,
   Sweet flower! I love, in forest bare,
To meet thee, when thy faint perfume
   Alone is in the virgin air.

Of all her train, the hands of Spring
   First plant thee in the watery mould;
And I have seen thee blossoming
   Beside the snow-bank's edges cold.

Thy parent sun, who bade thee view
   Pale skies, and chilling moisture sip,
Has bathed thee in his own bright hue,
   And streaked with jet thy glowing lip

Yet slight thy form, and low thy seat,
   And earthward bent thy gentle eye,
Unapt thy passing view to meet,
   When loftier flowers are flaunting nigh.

Oft in the sunless April day,
   Thy early smile has stay'd my walk;
But 'midst the gorgeous bloom of May,
   I pass'd thee on thy humble stalk.

8*

So they who climb to wealth forget
  The friends in darker fortunes tried:
I copied them — but I regret
  That I should ape the ways of pride.

And when again the genial hour
  Awakes the painted tribes of ligh.,
I 'll not o'erlook the modest flower
  That made the woods of April bright.

———

TO A WHITE VIOLET.

H. I. JOHNS.

Cox inmate of the lowly shade,
  'Mid clustering leaves embosom'd deep,
Why thus, in modest garb array'd,
  Hid'st thou beneath the hedge-row's steep?

While gaudier flowers that woo the sun,
  In all the pride of colour glow,
Thy odoriferous breath alone,
  Reveals the gem that lurks below.

So modest worth in humble guise,
  Retiring, shuns the gazing eye;
While round the hallow'd spot arise
  A thousand sweets that never die!

THE. VIOLET.

MISS LANDON.

WHY bettei than the lady rose,
　Loye I this little flower?
Because its fragrant leaves are those
　I loved in childhood's hour.

Though many a flower may win my praise
　The Violet has my love;
I did not pass my childish days
　In garden or in grove:

My garden' was the window-seat,
　Upon whose edge was set
A little vase, — the fair, the sweet, —
　It was the Violet.

It was my pleasure and my pride: —
　How I did watch its growth!
For health and bloom what plans I tried,
　And often injured both.

I placed it in the summer shower,
　I placed it in the sun;
And ever, at the evening hour,
　My work seem'd half undone.

The broad leaves spread, the small buds grew
　How slow they seem'd to be:
At last there came a tinge of blue, —
　'T was worth the world to me.

At length the perfume fill'd the room,
　Shed from the purple wreath;
No flower has now so rich a bloom,
　Has now so sweet a breath.

I gather'd two or three,—they seem'd
　Such rich gifts to bestow,—
So precious in my sight, I deem'd
　That all must think them so.

Ah! who is there but would be fain
　To be a child once more,
If future years could bring again
　All that they brought before?

My heart's world has been long o'erthrown,
　It is no more of flowers;—
Their bloom is past, their breath is flown,
　Yet I recall those hours.

Let Nature spread her loveliest,
　By spring or summer nurst;
Yet still I love the Violet best,
　Because I loved it first.

THE CROCUS.

SOME derive the name of this flower from a beautiful youth named Crocus, who is said to have been consumed by the ardour of his affection for Smilax; and afterwards metamorphosed into the plant which still bears his name. Others suppose it to be taken from Coriscus, a city and mountain of Cilicia.

The Spring Crocus is common in various parts of Europe: there are many varieties; and as this kind furnishes the florists with seed, new varieties continually occur. The most usual are the Common Yellow, Great Yellow, Deep Blue, Light Blue, White with Blue Stripes, Blue with White Stripes, White with a Purple Base, and Cream-coloured,—all natives of Britain: as also several from Scotland; the Black and White Striped, Cloth of Gold, &c.

The Yellow is the most showy for the garden, and the Purple the most beautiful; the White the most conspicuous, and the most curious.

If the season be mild, this plant will sometimes flower in February, and continue to enliven the parterre until April.

Crocus and Smilax may be turn'd to flowers,
And the Curetes spring from bounteous showers
I pass a hundred legends stale as these,
And with sweet novelty your taste will please.

OVID.

(89)

AND sudden Hyacinths the turf bestrow,
And flowery Crocus made the mountain glow.

HOMER

THE CROCUS.

J. R. PRIOR.

DAINTY young thing
Of life!—thou vent'rous flower,
Who growest through the hard, cold bower
Of wintry spring:—

Thou various-hued,
Soft, voiceless bell, whose spire
Rocks in the grassy leaves like wire,
In solitude;—

Like patience, thou
Art quiet in thy earth,
Instructing Hope that Virtue's birth
Is Feeling's vow.

Thy fancied bride!—
The delicate Snow-drop, keeps
Her home with thee; she wakes and sleeps
Near thy true side.

Will man but hear!
A simple flower can tell
What beauties in his mind should dwell
Through Passion's sphere.

THE AUTUMNAL CROCUS.

HOWITT.

THY bower, with vine unshaded,
　Stands desolate and lone;
The flowers of spring have faded,
　The summer birds are flown.
Thy home — whose claims are stronger
　Than time can e'er efface;
Thy garden — thine no longer —
　Have lost each look of grace:
For the stranger's foot has gone there, and left a ruin'd
　place.

The past came o'er my spirit —
　Thy kindness, and thy faith;
And must *thou* grief inherit,
　And life's undreamed-of scathe?
Is it *thou* — the gentlest, fairest,
　Like man must nerve thy heart,
And teach him how thou darest
　Meet fortune's keenest dart;
Then look on all thou loved from youth, and patiently
　depart?

'T was so : in vain I sought thee
   Within my garden-bower ;
And from the fields I brought thee, —
   Pale autumn's faithful flower.
Spring flowers, like fortune's lightness,
   With calm skies pass away :
But this reveals its brightness
   'Mid silence and decay ;
Like thy pure steadfast spirit, strong in sorrow's darkest
   day.

LILIES.

WE usually associate the idea of extreme whiteness with the Lily, so that it is common to express a pure white by comparison with the flower, as with snow: but Lilies, it is well known, are of almost every variety of colour.

The Common White Lily has been cultivated in England time immemorial. The stem is usually about three feet high. The flowers, which appear in June and July, are brilliantly white, and glossy on the inside. It is from the east; and in Japan the blossom is said to be nearly a span in length.

There are several varieties of the White Lily: as, that, with the flowers striped or blotched with purple; that with the leaves striped or edged with yellow; one with double, and one with pendulous flower.

Catesby's Lily was named in honour of Mr. Catesby who first found it in South Carolina. This flower, which blows in July and August, and is little more than a foot high, is variously shaded with red, orange, and lemon colours, and has no scent.

The Orange Lily, of which there are several varieties of species, has a large and brilliant flower, figured and dotted with black, and very red.

THE lady Lily, looking gently down.

The Lily, of all children of the spring
The palest — fairest too where fair ones are.

———— In virgin beauty blows
The tender Lily, languishingly sweet.

QUEEN of the field, in milk-white mantle drest,
The lovely Lily waved her curling crest.

———— and sweetest to the view,
The Lily of the vale, whose virgin flower
Trembles at every breeze, beneath its leafy bower

BARTON

———— the nice-leaved lesser Lilies,
Shading, like detected light,
Their little green-tipt lamps of white.

L. HUNT.

No flower amid the garden fairer grows
Than the sweet Lily of the lowly vale,
The queen of flowers.

Take but the humblest Lily of the field;
And if our pride will to our reason yield,
It must by sure comparison be shown,
That on the regal seat great David's son,
Array'd in all his robes and types of pow'r,
Shines with less glory than that simple flower.

TO LILIES.

ANON.

Where yonder *Lilies* wanton with the air,
  And no autumnal blasts have blown to fade,
  If flow'rs thou seek'st a festive wreath to braid,
Bend thy search thither, thou wilt find them there. —
Not in the arches of the forest, where
  The branching oaks extend unmoving shade;
The earth beyond their twisted roots is bare,
Save when perchance the *hop*, with tendrils curl'd,
Or *ivy* stringed, may seek and twine around
  Some stems amidst the forest chiefs that tower:
So, in the mightiest landscapes of the world,
  The *flowers of joy and love* are seldom found
  At the stern feet of knowledge or of power.

THE LILY.

PERCIVAL.

I had found out a sweet green spot,
  Where a Lily was blooming fair!
The din of the city disturb'd it not,
But the spirit, that shaded the quiet cot
With its wings of love, was there.

9*

I found that Lily's bloom,
When the day was dark and chill:
It smiled like a star in the misty gloom
And it sent abroad a soft perfume,
Which is floating around me still.

I sat by the Lily's bell,
And watch'd it many a day;
The leaves that rose in a flowing swell,
Grew faint and dim, then droop'd and fell,
And the flower had flown away.

I look'd where the leaves were laid,
In withering frailness, by,
And as gloomy thoughts stole on me, said,
There is many a sweet and blooming maic
Who will soon as dimly die.

———

THE LILY OF THE VALLEY AND THF ANEMONE

ANON.

Sweet flower, you fondly strive to hide
  Your lovely form from public view,
While the gay blossom's eastern pride
  Appears in every varied hue.

So will a cultured feeling mind,
  Oft, trembling, shrink from worldly gaze,
Whilst flippant wit, at ease reclined,
  Spreads all around its transient rays.

Yet do I love that modest flower
　　Which blossoms in the humble shade,
And asks not for the sun's bright power,
　　By which this splendid plant's array'd.

SONG OF THE LILY.

ANON.

Let others boast, in their golden pride,
Of graceful form, or roseate bloom —
Yet the Lily is fairer than all beside,
That glow in their beauty, or breathe in perfume.
What, though the bright Rose in her glory essay
To adorn with her blushes the cheek of the fair !
Yet no envied trophy can she bear away
For the Lily is ever her partner there.—
No triumph I fear from such rivals as these,
While gaily I wave my white bells to the breeze.

If the emblem of innocence homage commands,
Then what greater claim can the Lily desire?
For who will deny it — while radiant she stands,
Like the bright form of beauty, in bridal attire?
But I seek not the triumph of beauty alone —
Though the Rose may be foster'd 'neath Britain s proud
　　glance,
I shall still be her rival in glory's bright throne;
For who shall dare challenge the Lily of France?
While I can exult in such honours as these,
How proudly I'll wave my white bells in the breeze!

THE WATER-LILY.

MRS. HEMANS.

OH, beautiful thou art,
Thou sculpture-like and stately River-queen!
Crowning the depths, as with the light serene
    Of a pure heart.

    Bright Lily of the wave!
Rising in fearless grace with every swell,
Thou seem'st as if a spirit meekly brave
    Dwelt in thy cell:

    Lifting alike thy head,
Of placid beauty, feminine yet free,
Whether with foam or pictured azure spread
    The waters be.

    What is like thee, fair flower,
The gentle and the firm? thus bearing up
To the blue sky that alabaster cup,
    As to the shower?

    Oh! Love is most like thee,
The love of Woman; quivering to the blast
Through every nerve, yet rooted deep and fast
    'Midst Life's dark sea.

And Faith — oh! is not Faith
Like thee, too, Lily? springing into light,
Still buoyantly, above the billows' might,
    Through the storm's breath?

    Yes, link'd with such high thoughts,
Flower, let thine image in my bosom lie!
Till something there of its own purity
    And peace be wrought.

    Something yet more divine
Than the clear, pearly, virgin lustre shed
Forth· from thy breast upon the river's bed,
    As from a shrine.

THE TULIP.

This gay flower having been obtained from the Turks, was called Tulipa, from the resemblance of its corolla to the eastern head-dress called Tulipan or Turban, and hence our name of Tulip. To this resemblance Moore alludes in the following lines :—

> "What triumph crowds the rich Divan to-day
> With turban'd heads of every hue and race,
> Bowing before that veil'd and awful face,
> Like *Tulip-beds* of different shape and dyes,
> Bending beneath th' invisible west wind's sighs?"

The Garden Tulip is a native of the Levant; Linnæus says, of Cappadocia. It is very common in Syria, and is supposed by some persons, to be the Lily of the Field alluded to by Jesus Christ. It is said to have been introduced into England about the year 1580; for Hakluyt thus writes in 1582, "now within these four years there have been brought in England, from Vienna in Austria, divers kinds of flowers called Tulipas.'

THE *Tulip*, whose red veins
Are flush'd with deeper, warmer stains,
Glows in each leaf with more than Nimrod's fires.

ANON.

Down the *Tulip's* moisten'd cheek,
Spread with Nature's warmest bloom,
Sparkling drops of dew distil.

ANON.

THEN comes the Tulip race, where beauty plays
Her idle freaks : from family diffused
To family, as flies the father dust,
The varied colours run ; and while they break
On the charm'd eye, th' exulting florist marks,
With secret pride, the wonders of his hand.

THOMSON.

THE TULIP.

KLEIST.

WHO thus, *O Tulip!* thy gay-painted breast
In all the colours of the sun has drest?
Well could I call thee, in thy gaudy pride,
The Queen of flow'rs ; but blooming by thy side
Her thousand leaves that beams of love adorn,
Her throne surrounded by protecting thorn,
And smell eternal, form a juster claim,
Which gives the heaven-born *Rose* the lofty name,
Who, having slept throughout the wintry storm,
Now through the op'ning buds displays her smiling form.

SONG OF THE TULIP.

HOLLAND.

How vain are the struggles for conquest and power,
With golden bud and scented flower,
Who claim, from their beauty or fragrance alone,
Their right to ascend the garden throne ! —
A graceful form may please the sight,
And fragrant odour the senses delight ;

Yet, if we are judged by our merit, I ween
The Tulip will soon be the Garden Queen.—
No envy I fear, nor of beauty the frown,
While the worth of the Tulip can purchase the crown.

How can the vain Rose ever hope to claim,
By the verse of the poet, the bright meed of fame?
Or the pale-featured Lily pretend to enhance
Her right, as the flower most favour'd of France?
No favours I boast, though in beauty I shine,
And variety's garb, ever charming, is mine;
But my triumph I rest upon merit alone,
For worth is e'er valued when beauty is flown,
Then why should I fear either anger or frown,
While the worth of the Tulip will merit the crown?

THE ROSE

THE different kinds of Roses are quite numerous; and botanists find it very difficult to determine with accuracy which are species and which are varieties. On this account, Linnæus, and some other eminent authors, are inclined to think that there is only one real species of Rose, which is the Rosa Canina, or Dog-rose of the hedges, &c., and that all the other sorts are accidental varieties of it. However according to the Linnæan arrangement, they stand divided into fourteen species, each comprehending varieties, which in some sorts are but few, in others numerous.

Poetry is lavish of Roses: it heaps them into beds, weaves them into crowns, twines them into arbours, forges them into chains, and plants them in the bosom of beauty. It not only delights to bring in the Rose itself upon every occasion, but seizes each particular beauty it possesses as an object of comparison with the loveliest works of Nature; — as soft as a Rose leaf; as sweet as a Rose; Rosy Clouds; &c. &c

The eastern poets have united the Rose with the nightin-gale — the Venus of Flowers with the Apollo of birds.— The Rose is supposed to burst forth from its bud at the song of the nightingale.

- - - -

I saw the sweetest flower wild Nature yields,
A fresh-blown Musk Rose.

ANON.

A bed of Lilies flower upon her cheek,
And in the midst was set a circling Rose.

P. FLETCHER.

Its velvet lips the bashful Rose began
To show, and catch the kisses of the sun:
Some fuller blown, their crimson honours shed;
Sweet smelt the golden chives that graced their head

FAWKES.

THE lady Lily, paler than the moon,
And Roses, laden with the breath of June.

BARRY CORNWALL.

THERE was the pouting Rose, both red and white.

ANON.

AND first of all the Rose; because its breath
Is rich beyond the rest; and when it dies
It doth bequeath a charm to sweeten death.

BARRY CORNWALL.

AND thou, most lovely Rose,
Of tint most delicate,
Fair consort of the morn;
Delighted to imbibe
The genial dew of heaven,
Rich vegetation's vermeil-tinctured gem
April's enchanting herald,
Thou flower supremely blest,
And queen of all the flowers,
Thou formest around my locks

A garland of such fragrance,
That up to heaven itself
Thy balmy sweets ascend.

ANDREIN'S ' ADAM.'

His queen, the garden-queen, — his Rose,
Unbent by winds, unchill'd by snows,
Far from the winters of the west,
By every breeze and season blest,
Returns the sweets by Nature given
In softest incense back to heaven,
And grateful yields that smiling sky
Her fairest hue and fragrant sigh.

LORD BYRON.

Look as the flower which lingeringly doth fade,
The morning's darling mate, the Summer's queen
Spoil'd of that juice which kept it fresh and green.
As high as it did raise, bows low the head.

DRUMMOND

A single Rose is shedding there
Its lonely lustre, meek and pale:
It looks as planted by despair—
So white, so faint, the slightest gale
Might whirl the leaves on high;
And yet, though storms and blasts assail.
And hands more rude than wintry sky,
May wring it from the stem in vain—
To-morrow sees it bloom again!

The stalk some spirit quickly rears,
And waters with celestial tears;
   For well may maids of Helle deem
That this can be no earthly flower,
Which mocks the tempest's withering hour,
And buds unshelter'd by a bower;
Nor droops though Spring refuse her shower,
   Nor wooes the Summer beam:
To it the livelong night there sings
A bird unseen, but not remote;
Invisible his airy wings,
But soft as harp that Houri strings,
      His lone entrancing note.

BRIDE OF ABYDOS.

YONDER is a girl who lingers
Where wild honeysuckle grows,
Mingling with the Briar-rose;
And with eager outstretch'd fingers,
Tip-toe standing, vainly tries
To reach the hedge-enveloped prize.

H. SMITH.

WOUND in the hedge-rows' oaken boughs
The woodbine's tassels float in air,
And, blushing, the uncultured Rose
Hangs high her beauteous blossoms there.

SMITH

INVITATION TO A ROSE.

SMITH.

QUEEN of fragrance, lovely Rose,
The beauties of thy leaves disclose!
The winter's past, the tempests fly,
Soft gales breathe gently through the sky;
The lark, sweet warbling on the wing,
Salutes the gay return of Spring;
The silver dews, the vernal showers,
Call forth a bloomy waste of flowers;
The joyous fields, the shady woods,
Are clothed with green, or swell'd with buas.
Then haste thy beauties to disclose,
Queen of fragrance, lovely Rose!

The same. — ANON.

NURSED by the zephyr's balmy sigh,
    And cherish'd by the tears of morn;
Oh, queen of flowers! awake! arise!
    Oh haste, delicious Rose, be born!

Unheeding wish! no — yet awhile,
    Be yet awhile thy dawn delay'd;
Since the same hour that sees thee smile
    In orient bloom, shall see thee fade.

The same. — BOWRING.

ROSE of the morning, in thy glowing beauty,
Bright as the stars, and delicate and lovely,

Lift up thy head above thy earthly dwelling,
   Daughter of heaven!

Wake! for the watery clouds are all dispersing!
Zephyr invites thee: frosts and snows of winter
All are departed; and Favonian breezes
   Welcome thee, smiling.

ON AN EARLY ROSE.

ANON.

Sweet Rose, whom early showers
   Have kindly, fondly nurst:
I love thy leaves of red,
For from fair Flora's bed
Thou lift'st thy modest head,
   Sweet Rose—the *First*.

What spell is in that word,
   The *First!* the primal one:
Oh! wherefore loves to stray
The mind to pleasure's day,
And count in life's pathway
   The sweets that shone!

Is it because of joys
   Long since like dreams are fled,
Though each had rapture in it,
None had that charm within it,
As when that First—*First* minute,
   Their sweets were shed?

THE MOSS ROSE.

FROM THE GERMAN.

THE Angel of the flowers, one day,
Beneath a Rose-tree sleeping lay —
That spirit to whom charge is given
To bathe young buds in dews of heaven;
Awaking from his light repose,
The Angel whisper'd to the Rose:
"O fondest object of my care,
"Still fairest found where all are fair,
"For the sweet shade thou giv'st to me;
"Ask what thou wilt, 't is granted thee!"

"Then," said the Rose, with deepen'd glow,
"On me another grace bestow!" —
The spirit paused in silent thought, —
What grace was there that flower had not?
'T was but a moment — o'er the Rose
A veil of moss the angel throws;
And, robed in Nature's simplest weed,
Could there a flower that Rose exceed?

THE WILD ROSE.

MILLHOUSE.

OH! there's a wild Rose in yon rugged dell,
    Fragrant as that which blooms the garden's pride
And there's a sympathy no tongue can tell,
    Breathed from the linnet chanting by its side:

And there is music in that whispering rill,
  Far more delightsome than the raging main;
And more of beauty on yon verdant hill,
  Than to the grandest palace can pertain:
For there is nought so lovely and serene,
  Throughout the chambers of the mightiest king,
As the pure calm that rests upon this scene,
  'Mid sporting lambkins and the songs of spring:
Yet oft, attracted by some dazzling show,
  Man flies from peace, pursuing gilded woe.

THE FADING ROSE.

C. J. FOX.

THE *Rose*, the sweetly-blooming *Rose*,
  Ere from the tree it's torn,
Is like the charms which Beauty shows,
  In life's exulting morn.

But. oh! how soon its sweets are gone,
  How soon it withering lies!
So when the eve of life comes on.
  Sweet Beauty fades and dies.

Then, since the fairest form that's made
  Soon withering we shall find
Let us possess what ne'er will fade, —
  The beauties of the *Mind*.

THE EVERLASTING ROSE.

ANSTER.

HAIL to thy hues! thou lovely flower;
  Still shed around thy soft perfume,
Still smile amid the wintry hour,
  And boast even now a spring-tide bloom.

Thine is, methinks, a pleasing dream,
  Lone lingerer in the icy vale,
Of smiles that hail'd the morning beam,
  And sighs more sweet for evening's gale.

Still are thy green leaves whispering
  Low sounds to fancy's ear, that tell
Of mornings, when the wild bee's wing
  Shook dew-drops from thy sparkling cell!

In April's bower thy sweets are breathed,
  And June beholds thy blossoms fair;
In Autumn's chaplet thou art wreathed,
  And round December's forehead bare.

With thee the graceful Lily vied,
  As Summer breezes waved her head,
And now the Snow-drop at thy side
  Meekly contrasts thy cheerful red.

'Tis thine to hear each varying voice,
  That marks the seasons sad or gay,
The summer thrush bids thee rejoice
  And wintry robin's dearer lay.

Sweet flower! how happy dost thou seem
 'Mid parching heat, 'mid nipping frost,—
While gathering beauty from each beam,
 No hue, no grace of thine is lost!

Thus Hope, 'mid life's severest days,
 Still smiles, still triumphs o'er despair :
Alike she lives in Pleasure's rays,
 And cold Affliction's winter air.

Charmer alike in lordly bower,
 And in the hermit's cell, she glows :
The Poet's and the Lover's flower,
 The bosom's Everlasting Rose!

SHARON'S ROSE.

ANON.

Go, Warrior, pluck the laurel bough,
And bind it round thy reeking brow :
Ye sons of pleasure! blithely twine
A chaplet of the purple vine ;
And Beauty cull each blushing flower
That ever deck'd the sylvan bower;
No wreath is bright, no garland fair,
Unless sweet Sharon's Rose be there.

The laurel branch will droop and die,
The vine its purple fruit deny,
The wreath that smiling beauty twined
Will leave no lingering bud behind;

For beauty's wreath, and beauty's bloom,
In vain would shun the withering tomb,
Where nought is bright and nought is fair,
Unless sweet Sharon's Rose be there.

Bright blossom! of immortal bloom,
Of fadeless hue, and sweet perfume,
Far in the desert's dreary waste
In lone neglected beauty placed,—
Let others seek the blushing bower,
And cull the frail and fading flower,
But I 'll to dreariest wilds repair,
If Sharon's deathless Rose be there.

When Nature's hand with cunning care,
No more the opening bud shall rear,
But, hurl'd by heaven's avenging Sire,
Descends the earth-consuming fire,
And desolation's hurrying blast,
O'er all the sadden'd scene has past,
There is a clime for ever fair,
And Sharon's Rose shall flourish there.

11

THE WALL-FLOWER.

The common Wall-flower is a native of the South of Eu
rope, and is found wild in Switzerland, France, and Spain,
and we may infer, that it was one of the earliest flowers
which was cultivated in gardens, from its being so constantly found on the ruins of old buildings.

The Wall-flowers which grow out of the crevices of old
buildings are of a much hardier nature than those of the
garden; for as they can receive but little moisture by the
fibres of their roots, their stem becomes firm and woody,
and able to bear the frost without injury, whereas those cultivated in the garden become succulent, and consequently
more susceptible of cold. The two principal varieties of the
Wall-flower are the yellow, and the red or bloody.

The rude stone fence, with Wall-flowers gay,
To me more pleasure yield
Than all the pomp imperial domes display.

SCOTT.

And well the lonely infant knew
Recesses where the Wall-flower grew,
And honey-suckle loved to crawl,
Up the low crag and ruin'd wall.
I deem'd such nooks the sweetest shade
The sun in all his round survey'd;

And still I thought that shatter'd tower
The mightiest work of human power.

SCOTT.

TO THE WALL-FLOWER.

ANON.

I WILL not praise the often-flatter'd Rose
  Or virgin-like, with blushing charms half seen,
  Or when in dazzling splendour, like a queen,
All her magnificence of state she shows;
No, nor that nun-like Lily, which but blows
  Beneath the valley's cool and shady screen;
  Nor yet the Sun-flower, that with warrior mien,
Still eyes the orb of glory where it glows;—
But thou, neglected *Wall-flower*, to my breast
  And muse art dearest, wildest, sweetest flower,
To whom alone the privilege is given
  Proudly to root thyself above the rest
As genius does, and, from thy rocky tower,
  Send fragrance to the purest breath of heaven

THE WALL-FLOWER.

DELTA.

THE Wall-flower — the Wall-flower,
How beautiful it blooms!
It gleams above the ruin'd tower,
Like sun-light over tombs;

It sheds a halo of repose
Around the wrecks of Time:
To beauty give the flaunting Rose, —
The Wall-flower is sublime.

Flower of the solitary place!
Grey Ruin's golden crown!
That lendest melancholy grace
To haunts of old renown:
Thou mantlest o'er the battlement,
By strife or storm decay'd;
And fillest up each envious rent
Time's canker-tooth hath made.

Thy roots outspread the ramparts o'er
    Where, in war's stormy day,
The Douglases stood forth of yore
    In battle's grim array:
The clangour of the field is fled,
    The beacon on the hill
No more through midnight blazes red —
    But thou art blooming still!

Whither hath fled the choral band
    That fill'd the abbey's nave?
Yon dark sepulchral yew trees stand
    O'er many a level grave:
In the belfry's crevices the dove
    Her young brood nurseth well,
Whilst thou, lone flower, dost shed above
    A sweet decaying smell.

In the season of the Tulip-cup,
  When blossoms clothe the trees,
How sweet to throw the lattice up,
  And scent thee on the breeze:
The butterfly is then abroad,
  The bee is on the wing,
And on the hawthorn by the road
  The linnets sit and sing.

Sweet Wall-flower, sweet Wall-flower!
  Thou conjurest up to me
Full many a soft and sunny hour
  Of boyhood's thoughtless glee,
When joy from out the daisies grew,
  In woodland pastures green,
And summer skies were far more blue
  Than since they e'er have been.

Now Autumn's pensive voice is heard
  Amid the yellow bowers,
The robin is the regal bird,
  And thou the Queen of Flowers!
He sings on the laburnum trees,
  Amid the twilight dim,
And Araby ne'er gave the breeze
  Such scenes as thou to him.

Rich is the Pink, the Lily gay,
  The Rose is Summer's guest;
Bland are the charms when these **decay**
  Of flowers first, last, and best!
11*

There may be gaudier on the bower,
 And statelier on the tree,
But Wall-flower, loved Wall-flower,
 Thou art the flower for me.

The same. — TOWNSEND.

THE Rose and Lily blossom fair,
 But all unmeet for Sorrow's child;
They deck the bower and gay parterre,
 As if for Mirth alone they smiled.

The *Cowslip* nods upon the lea;
 And, where wild wreaths the green lanes dress,
The Woodbine blooms, but not for me,
 For these are haunts of Happiness.

I will not seek the mossy bed,
 Where *Violets* court soft vernal showers,
For Quiet there reclines her head,
 And Innocence is gathering flowers.

The WALL-FLOWER only shall be mine·
 Its simple faith is dear to me·
To roofless tower, and prostrate shrine,
 It clings with patient constancy

And, prodigal of love, blooms on,
 Though all unseen its beauties die,
And, though for desert gales alone,
 Breathes fragrance rich as Araby.

Oh, there appears a generous scorn
  Of all requital in its choice!
The thousand flowers that earth adorn,
  In earth's exuberant stores rejoice.

It only asks the freshening dew,
  Imparting all where nought is given —
Raised above earth, as if it drew
  Its only nutriment from heaven.

THE HYACINTH, OR HAREBELL.

THE common, or Wood Hyacinth, is a native of Per sia, and of many parts of Europe. In the spring it abounds in our woods, hedges, &c.; and on this account the old botanists have given it the name of the English Hyacinth. The botanic designation of Hyacintus non-scriptus is applied to it because it has not the Ai on the petals, and .herefore is not the poetical Hyacinth.

THE Harebell, for her stainless, azure hue,
Claims to be worn by none but those are true.

Blue-bell! how gaily art thou drest,
   How neat and trim art thou, sweet flower,
How silky is thy azure vest,
   How fresh to flaunt at morning's hour!
Could'st thou but *think*, I well might say
Thou art as proud in rich array
As lady, blithesome, young, and vain,
Prank'd up with folly and disdain,
Vaunting her power.
              Sweet flower!

MRS. ROBINSON.

(190)

The same.— ANON.

SWEET Flower! though many a ruthless storm
Sweep fiercely o'er thy slender form,
And many a sturdier plant may bow
In death beneath the tempest's blow,
Submissive thou, in pensive guise,
Uninjured by each gale, shalt rise,
And deck'd with innocence remain
The fairest tenant of the plain :
So, conscious of its lowly state,
Trembles the heart assail'd by fate,
Yet, when the fleeting blast is o'er,
Settles as transient as before ;
While the proud breast no peace shall find.
No refuge for a troubled mind.

THE HAREBELL AND THE FOX-GLOVE.

ANON.

 a valley obscure, on a bank of green shade,
A sweet little Harebell her dwelling had made ;
Her roof was a Woodbine, that tastefully spread
Its close-woven tendrils, o'erarching her head :
Her bed was of moss, that each morning made new ;
She dined on a sunbeam and supp'd on the dew :
Her neighbour, the nightingale, sung her to rest ;
And care had ne'er planted a thorn in her breast.

One morning she saw, on the opposite side,
A Fox-glove displaying his colours of pride:
She gazed on his form, that in stateliness grew,
And envied his height, and his brilliant hue;
She mark'd how the flow'rets all gave way before him,
While they press'd round her dwelling with far less
    decorum :
Dissatisfied, jealous, and peevish she grows,
And the sight of this Fox-glove destroys her repose.

She tires of her vesture, and, swelling with spleen,
Cries " Ne'er such a dowdy blue mantle was seen!"
Nor keeps to herself any longer her pain,
But thus to a primrose begins to complain:
" I envy your mood, that can patient abide,
' The respect paid that Fox-glove, his airs, and his pride:
" There you sit, still the same, with your colourless cheek;
" But you have no spirit — would I were as meek!"

The Primrose, good-humour'd, replied, " If you knew
" More about him — (remember I'm older than you,
" And, better instructed, can tell you his tale)
" You'd envy him least of all flowers in the vale:
" With all his fine airs and his dazzling show,
" No blossom more baneful and odious can blow;
" And the reason that flow'rets before him give way
" Is because they all hate him and shrink from his sway

" To stay near him long would be fading or death,
" For he scatters a pest with his venomous breath;

" While the flowers that you fancy are crowding you there
" Spring round you, delighted your converse to share :
" His flame-colour'd robe is imposing, 't is true;
" Yet, who likes it so well as your mantle of blue !
" For we know that of innocence one is the vest;
" The other the cloak of a treacherous breast.

" I see your surprise — but I know him full well,
" And have number'd his victims, as fading they fell :
" He blighted twin Violets that under him lay,
" And poison'd a sister of mine the same day !"
The Primrose was silent — The Harebell, 't is said,
Inclined for a moment her beautiful head ;
But quickly recovered her spirits, and then
Declared that she ne'er should feel envy again.

THE CEREUS.

THE night-flowering Cereus (Cactus grandi-florus,) is one of our most splendid hot-house plants, and is a native of Jamaica and some other of the West India Islands. Its stem is creeping, and thickly set with spines. The flower is white and very large, sometimes nearly a foot in diameter. Its petals are of a pure and dazzling white; and a vast number of recurved stamens, surrounding the style in the centre, add to its beauty. The fine scent of this extraordinary flower perfumes the air to a considerable distance; but the most remarkable circumstance with regard to it, is the short time which it takes to expand, and the rapidity with which it decays. Upon large plants, eight or ten flowers will open on the same night, making a most magnificent appearance by candlelight, bloom for an hour or more, then begin to droop, and before morning be completely dead. This plant does not bear fruit in this country, and must be nursed in a stove to enable it to produce flowers.

THE NIGHT-BLOWING CEREUS

ANON.

Can it be true? so fragrant and so fair!
To give thy perfume to the dews of night?
Can aught so beautiful shrink from the glare,
And fade and sicken in the coming light?

Yes, peerless flower! the heavens alone exnale
Thy fragrance, while the glittering stars attest;
And incense, wafted from the midnight gale,
Untainted rises from thy spotless breast.
Sweet emblem of that faith, which seeks, apart
From human praise, to love and work unseen;
That gives to Heaven an undivided heart —
In sorrow steadfast, and in joy serene!
Anchor'd on GOD, no adverse cloud can dim;
Her eye, unalter'd, still is fix'd on Him!

TO THE NIGHT-BLOWING CEREUS.

H. I. JOHNS.

FLOWER of the Night! mysteriously awake
When Earth's green tribes repose, why stealthful thus
Comest thou to meet the stars — unfolding soft,
Beneath their tranquil ray, thy peerless form?
Flower of the night! chaster than Alpine snows —
Unvisited by aught save Heaven's sweet breath —
Why hide thy loveliness from mortal eye,
Why pour thy fragrance to the unconscious night?
— Thou art, alas! too exquisitely fair,
Too pure for Earth's corrupted denizens!
Yet not in vain thy odoriferous breath,
And beauty all unearthly: *He* who thus
Hath fashion'd thee a chaste and midnight gem;

Who stamp'd thee with the lincaments of grace,
But veil'd thy birth and short-lived bloom in darkness
Some end beneficent design'd, though far
Beyond or human ken or comprehension! —
Earth's lowliest herb is eloquent of *Him*,
The Great Supreme! and thou, mysterious flower
Fair glory of the night! might Fancy give
Thy voice interpretation, couldst unfold
Why form'd so fair, and why ordain'd to spend
Thy sweets nectareous in nocturnal gloom.

THE CELANDINE.

THE name of this plant is derived from the Greek, and signifies a swallow. It is not so named, as some have supposed, from its coming and going with the swallow; but, according to Gerard, from an opinion which prevailed among the country-people, that the old swallows used it to restore sight to their young when their eyes were out. For the same reason, it is also called Swallow-wort.

TO THE SMALL CELANDINE.

ANON.

PANSIES, Lilies, Kingcups, Daisies,
Let them live upon their praises;
Long as there's a sun that sets,
Primroses will have their glory;
Long as there are Violets,
They will have a place in story;
There's a flower that shall be mine,
'T is the little Celandine.

Eyes of some men travel far
For the finding of a star;
Up and down the heavens they go,
Men that keep a mighty rout!
I'm as great as they, I trow,
Since the day I found thee out:

Little flower!—I 'll make a stir,
Like a great Astronomer.

Modest, yet withal an elf,
Bold, and lavish of thyself;
Since we needs must first have met,
I have seen thee high and low,
Thirty years or more, and yet
'T was a face I did not know;
Thou hast now, go where I may,
Fifty greetings in a day.

Ere a leaf is on a bush,
In the time before the thrush
Has a thought about its nest,
Thou wilt come with half a call,
Spreading out thy glossy breast
Like a careless prodigal;
Telling tales about the sun,
When we 've little warmth or none.

Poets, vain men in their mood!
Travel with the multitude:
Never heed them; I aver,
That they all are wanton wooers;
But the thrifty cottager,
Who stirs little out of doors,
Joys to spy thee near her home—
Spring is coming, thou art come·

Comſort have thou of thy merit,
Kindly, unassuming spirit!
Careless of thy neighbourhood,
Thou dost show thy pleasant face
On the moor, and in the wood,
In the lane — there's not a place,
Howsoever mean it be,
But 't is good enough for thee.

Ill beſall the yellow flowers,
Children of the flaring hours!
Buttercups, that will be seen,
Whether we will see or no;
Others, too, of lofty mien:
They have done as worldlings do,
Taken praise that should be thine,
Little, humble Celandine!

Prophet of delight and mirth
Scorn'd and slighted upon earth!
Herald of a mighty band,
Of a joyous train ensuing,
Singing at my heart's command,
In the lanes my thoughts pursuing,
I will sing, as doth behove,
Hymns in praise of what I love!

12*

THE ORCHIS.

THE Greeks named this plant Orchis, from the form of the roots in many of the species; and this appellation is now generally adopted in most of the European languages. In addition to the Greek name, the Latins often call it Satyrion, because the early Romans believed it to be the food of the Satyrs, and that it excited them to the excesses which in fabulous history are ascribed to them. Its old English names are Standlewort and Kingfingers.

In consequence either of a want of taste in floriculture, or of a foolish predilection for an ient prejudices, this beautiful flower has been excluded from the parterre of Flora; but so anxious have been the Botanists to collec its different species from all quarters of the world, tha from their exertions we now possess upwards of eighty distinct species, besides numerous varieties of several of the kinds.

THE BEE ORCHIS.

R. SNOW, ESQ.

SEE, Delia, see this image bright!
Why starts my fair one at the sight?

It mounts not on obtrusive wing,
Nor threats thy breast with angry sting:
Admire, as close the insect lies,
Its thin-wrought plume and honey'd thighs:
Whilst on this flow'ret's velvet breast,
It seems as though 'twere lull'd to rest,
Nor might its fairy wings unfold,
Enchain'd in aromatic gold.
Think not to set the captive free —
'Tis but the picture of a bee.

Yet wonder not that Nature's power
Should paint an insect in a flower;
And stoop to means that bear in part
Resemblance to imperfect art —
Nature, who could that form inspire
With strength and swiftness, life and fire,
And bid it search each spicy vale
Where flowers their fragrant souls exhale;
And, labouring for the parent hive,
With murmurs make the wild alive.

For when in Parian stone we trace
Some best-remember'd form or face;
Or see on radiant canvass rise
An imitative Paradise;
And feel the warm affections glow,
Pleased at the pencil's mimic show;

'T is but obedience to the plan
From Nature's birth proposed to Man;
Who, lest her choicest sweets in vain
Should blossom for our thankless train,
Lest beauty pass unheeded by
Like cloud upon the summer sky;
Lest mem'ry of the brave and just
Should sleep with them consign'd to dust:
With leading hand th' expedient proves,
And paints for us the form she loves.

THE ANEMONE.

ANEMONE is derived from the Greek ANEMOS, wind, as Gerard says, after Pliny, because 'the flower doth never open itself but when the wind doth blow.' As this is not quite correct, at least with the Anemone of our day, the appellation is supposed to have arisen from the plant flourishing in exposed and windy situations.

The ancient fabulists ascribe to this flower a very high birth. They tell us that Venus, in her grief for the death of Adonis, mingled her tears with his blood, and that thence sprung the first Anemone.

The Anemones are natives of the East, whence their roots were originally brought; but they have been so much improved by culture, as to take a high rank among the ornaments of our gardens in the spring.

————

SEE! yon Anemones their leaves unfold,
With rubies flaming, and with living gold.

ANON

Then, thickly strewn in woodland bowers,
Anemones their Stars unfold.

ANON.

Youth, like a thin Anemone, displays
His silken leaf, and in a morn decays.

And then I gather'd rushes, and began
To weave a garland for you, intertwined
With Violets, Hepaticas, Primroses,
And coy Anemone, that ne'er uncloses
Her lips until they're blown on by tne wind.

AMARYNTHUS.

TO THE WOOD-ANEMONE.

ANON.

WELCOME! though cold the hour,
           Anemone!
And shelterless the hazel be;
Yet Spring shall form the greener bower,
And sunshine bring, and warmer shower,
           To foster thee.

Where hast thou been since last
           The wanton air
Was roving through thy chambers fair?
Did elfin troop then close them fast,
And have the while, in revels past,
           Pavilioned there?

Ur hast thou been in quest
           Of Summer spot

To dwell upon, yet found it not?
Or here to strip thy beauteous vest,
And lay thee down like death to rest,
            Hath been thy lot?

Welcome! for drear the gale
            Has been to me,
And all the flow'rets wither'd be
Young life had rear'd in sun and shade,
They spring no more, though they do fade
            And die like thee.

Yet though this be the doom
            Of earthly flower,
And earthly hopes may feel its power,
Still hopes are left that mock the tomb,
And nurture here the strength to bloom
           In heavenly bower

PASSION-FLOWER.

THE Passion-flower derives its name from a superstitious idea that all the instruments of the Saviour's passion are represented in it.

Most of the Passion-flowers are natives of the hottest parts of America, and require a stove in more northern latitudes. It is a beautiful genus. The rose-coloured Passion-flower is a native of Virginia, and is the species which was first known in Europe. It has since been, in a great measure, superseded by the blue Passion-flower, which is hardy enough to flower in the open air, and makes an elegant tapestry for an unsightly wall. The leaves of this, in the autumn, are of the most brilliant crimson; and, when the sun is shining upon them, seem to transport one to the gardens of Pluto.

THE PASSION-FLOWER.

BARTON.

WE roam the seas — give new-found isles
  Some King's or Conqueror's name;
We rear on earth triumphal piles,
  As meeds of earthly fame.

Then may not *one* poor flow'ret's bloom
  The holier memory share,
Of him who, to avert our doom,
  Vouchsafed our sins to bear.

God dwelleth not in temples raised
   By work of human hands;
Yet shrines august, by men revered,
   Are found in Christian lands.

And may not e'en a simple flower
   Proclaim his glorious praise,
Whose fiat only had the power
   Its form from earth to raise?

Then freely let the blossoms ope,
   Its beauties to recall,
A scene which bids the humble hope
   In him who died for all.

The same. — DR. EDMUND CARTWRIGHT.

YON mystic flower, with gold and azure bright,
Whose stem luxuriant speaks a vigorous root,
Unfolds her blossoms to the morn's salute,
That close and die in the embrace of night.
No luscious *fruits* the cheated taste invite —
Her short-lived blossoms, ere they lead to fruit,
Demand a genial clime, and suns that shoot
Their rays direc', with undiminish'd light.
Thus HOPE, the passion-flower of human life,
Whose wild luxuriance mocks the pruner's knife,
Profuse in promise makes a like display
Of evanescent blooms — that last a day;
To cheer the mental eye no more is given:
The FRUIT is only to be found — in HEAVEN.

HAWTHORN.

Few trees exceed the common Hawthorn in beauty, during the season of its bloom. Its blossoms have been justly compared to those of the myrtle: they are admir able also for their abundance, and for their exquisite fra grance. This shrub usually flowers in May; and being the handsomest then (or perhaps at any time) wild in oui fields, has obtained the name of May, or May-bush. The country-people deck their houses and churches with the blossoms on May-day, as they do with Holly at Christmas

---

THE HAWTHORN.

ANON.

On Summer's breast the Hawthorn shines
   In all the Lily's bloom,
'Mid slopes where th' evening flock reclines.
   Where glows the golden broom.

When yellow Autumn decks the plain,
   The Hawthorn's boughs are green,
Amid the ripening fields of grain,
   In emerald brightness seen.

A night of frost, a day of wind
   Have stript the forest bare:
The Hawthorn too that blast shall find
   Nor shall that spoiling spare.

But, red with fruit, that Hawthorn bough,
  Though leafless, yet will shine;
The blackbird far its hues shall know,
  As lapwing knows the vine.

Be thus thy youth as Lilies gay,
  Thy manhood vigorous green;
And thus let fruit bedeck thy spray,
  'Mid age's leafless scene.

The same. — ANON.

FAIR Hawthorn flowering,
  With green shade bowering
Along the lovely shore;
    To thy foot around
    With his long arm wound
A wild vine has mantled thee o'er.

    In merry spring-tide,
    When to woo his bride
The nightingale comes again,
    Thy boughs among
    He warbles his song,
That lightens a lover's pain.

    'Mid thy topmost leaves
    His nest he weaves
Of moss and the satin fine,
    Where his callow brood
    Shall chirp at their food,
Secure from each hand but mine
13*

Gentle Hawthorn, thrive
And, for ever alive,
May'st thou blossom as now in thy prime;
By the wind unbroke,
And the thunderstroke,
Unspoil'd by the axe of time.

THE GENTIAN.

THIS genus of plant has received its name in honour of Gentius, a King of Illyria, who is said to have discovered one of the species of it. He is also supposed to have experienced its virtues on his army, as a cure for the plague.

The Gentians are very numerous, and many of them eminently beautiful. They are generally very difficult to preserve in a garden; and, being long-rooted, very few are adapted for planting in pots. The smaller kinds, however, may be so cultivated: as the Swallow-wort-leaved, which does not exceed a foot in height, and has large light-blue bell-shaped flowers, blowing in July and August. The roots only are perennial; the stalks decay annually: and of most of the species the flowers appear but once in two or three years. The March Gentian has also fine blue flowers, though few in number, and blows in August and September. This species grows naturally in England and many other parts of Europe

THE GENTIANELLA

MONTGOMERY.

IN LEAF.

GREEN thou art, obscurely green,
Meanest plant among the mean!
— From the dust *I* took my birth;
Thou too art a child of earth.
I aspire not to be great;
Scorn not thou my low estate:
Wait the time, and thou shalt see
Honour crown humility,
Beauty set her seal on me.

IN FLOWER.

Blue thou art, intensely blue!
Flower, whence came thy dazzling hue,
—When I open'd first mine eye,
Upward glancing to the sky,
Straightway from the firmament
Was the sapphire-brilliance sent:
Brighter glory wouldst thou share!
Look to heaven, and seek it there
In the act of faith and prayer.

The same.— MRS. SIGOURNEY.

MEEK dwellers 'mid yon terror-stricken cliffs!
With brows so pure, and incense-breathing lips,

Whence are ye?—Did some white-winged messenger
On Mercy's missions, trust your timid germ
To the cold cradle of eternal snows?
Or, breathing on the callous icicles,
Bid them with tear-drops nurse ye?—
                    —Tree nor shrub
Dare that drear atmosphere; no polar pine
Uprears a veteran front; yet there *ye* stand,
Leaning your cheeks against the thick-ribb'd ice,
And looking up with brilliant eyes to Him
Who bids you bloom unblanch'd amid the waste
Of desolation. Man, who, panting, toils
O'er slippery steeps, or, trembling, treads the verge
Of yawning gulfs, o'er which the headlong plunge
Is to eternity, looks shuddering up,
And marks ye in your placid loveliness—
Fearless, yet frail—and, clasping his chill hands
Blesses your pencill'd beauty. 'Mid the pomp
Of mountain summits, rushing on the sky,
And chaining the rapt soul in breathless awe,
He bows to bind you drooping to his breast,
Inhales your spirit from the frost-wing'd gale,
And freer dreams of heaven.

FORGET-ME-NOT, OR MYOSOTIS PALUSTRIS.

THIS plant is named Myosotis from mus, a rat, and ous otos, an ear. Its oval, velvety leaves are like the ears of a rat or mouse. It is a well-known sentimental flower: will grow everywhere; and varies more than most plants with situation. On dry walls and rubbish it is dwarfish, rough, and hairy, not rising when in flower more than two or three inches; in muddy ditches it is smooth all over, of a shining light green, and two or three feet high. In common soils, as in a garden, or loamy corn-field, it assumes an intermediate character.

FORGET-ME-NOT.

BERNARD BARTON.

BLOSSOMS more rich and rare than thou
May twine round Beauty's graceful brow
    In moods of sunny mirth;
The Rose's or the Myrtle's flower
Might more beseem her festive hour,
And give, in Pleasure's careless bower,
    To brighter fancies birth.

But in these moments sad, yet dear,
When parting wakes affection's tear,
    Thy stainless blossoms' braid,

Whose name forbids us to forget,
Would be the chosen coronet,
Love on the loveliest brow would set
　　To crave fond Memory's aid.

When, "earth to earth," and "dust to dust,"
The loved, lamented, we entrust,
　　What flower may grace the spot,
Where sleep the reliques of the dead,
For whom the frequent tear is shed,
Like thine — which, from the grave's cold bed,
　　Repeats "Forget-me-not?"

———

SONG OF THE FORGET-ME-NOT

ANON.

How many bright flowers now around me are glancing,
Each seeking its praise, or its beauty enhancing!
The Rose-buds are hanging like gems in the air
And the Lily-bell waves in her fragrance there.
　Alas! I can claim neither fortune nor power,
　Neither beauty nor fragrance are cast in my lot;
　But contented I cling to my lowly bower,
　And smile while I whisper — "*Forget-me-not!*"

The jasmine so lovely is o'er me entwining,
With the sweet-scented Violet its odours combining,—
May their discord be ended, and, smiling in peace,
Be it long ere their sweet dreams of happiness cease!

While I am contented to blossom apart,
In my humble bower, by the lowy cot,
I ask for no homage but that of the heart,
And smile while I whisper — " *Forget-me-not !*"

MOSSES.

A FEW of the most remarkable Mosses are, the Greater Water-moss, the Grey Bog-moss, the Yellow Powder-wort, and the Common Club-moss.

Mosses are almost constantly green, and have the finest verdure in autumn. Some of the Mosses spread in a continual leaf; others grow hollow above, like small cups; others round on the top, like mushrooms; and some shoot out in branches. All these have their different seeds. which do not require great delicacy of soil, but take root on any thing where they can grow unmolested. Those *Mosses* which rise immediately from the earth are more perfect: some of them white and hollow, or fistulous; and some of them not much inferior to regular plants. The more sorts grow on stones, in the form of a pile or fur, like velvet, and of a glossy colour, between green and black. But the first sort, which appears like scurf or crust, seems to rise but one degree above the unwrought mould or earth. An unhealthy tree is never without these imperfect *super-plants*, and the more unhealthy the tree is, the better they thrive.

THE MOSS.

Ah, lovely flower! what care, what power,
In thy fair structure are display'd,
By Him who rear'd thee to this hour,
Within the forest's lonely shade!

Thy tender stalk, and fibres fine,
Here find a shelter from the storm.
Perhaps no human eyes but mine
Ere gazed upon thy lovely form.

The dew-drop glistens on thy leaf,
As if thou seem'dst to shed a tear:
As if thou knew'st my tale of grief —
Felt all my sufferings severe.

But, ah! thou know'st not my distress,—
In danger here from beasts of prey,
And robb'd of all I did possess,
By men more fierce by far than they.

Nor canst thou ease my burden'd sigh,
Nor cool the fever at my heart,
Though to the zephyrs passing by
Thou dost thy balmy sweets impart.

Yet He that form'd thee, little plant,
And bade thee flourish in this place,
Who sees and feels my every want,
Can still support me by His grace.

Oft has His arm, all strong to save,
Protected my defenceless head
From ills I never could perceive,
Nor could my feeble hand have stay'd.

Then shall I still pursue my way
O'er the wild desert's sun-burnt soil,
To where the ocean's swelling spray
Washes my long'd-for native isle.

SUN-FLOWER, MARIGOLD, AND HELIOTROPE.

The Sun-flower does not derive its name, as some have supposed, from turning to the sun, but from the resemblance of the full-blown flower to the sun itself: Gerard remarks, that he has seen four of these flowers on the same stem, pointing to the four cardinal points. This flower is a native of Mexico and Peru, and looks as if it grew from their own gold. It flowers from June to October.

The principal species of Sun-flower are — the Dwarf Annual, the Perennial, the Dark Red, and the narrow-leaved.

Several of the Sun-flowers are natives of Canada, where they are much admired and cultivated by the inhabitants, in gardens, for their beauty; in the United States we sow whole acres of land with them, for the purpose of preparing oil from their seeds, of which they produce an immense number.

The Sun-flower was formerly called Marigold also, as the Marigold was termed Sun-flower. Gerard styles it the Sun marigold.

In old authors, the name for the plant, which is now more strictly and properly designated the Marigold, is Golds, or Rudds. Golds, or Gouldes, is a name given by the country-people to a variety of yellow flowers; and the name of the Virgin Mary has been added to many plants which were anciently, for their beauty, named after Venus, of which the Marigold is one: Costmary, the Virgin Mary's Costus, is another.

The Field Marigold is a native of most parts of Europe, and differs but little from the garden Marigold, except in being altogether smaller.

There are many varieties of the Garden Marigold; one of which, the Proliferous, called by Gerard the fruitful Marigold, is, as he says, 'called by the vulgar sort of women, Jack-an-apes on horseback.' Although this species of Marigold is generally yellow, there is a variety with purple flowers.

Linnæus has observed, that the Marigold is usually open from nine in the morning to three in the afternoon. This circumstance attracted early notice, and on this account the plant has been termed *Solisequa* (Sun-follower), and *Solis sponsa*, Spouse of the Sun.

The Heliotrope is the same with the Turnsole, both names being derived from words which signify to turn with the sun.

The Sun-flower is of the class *Syngenesia*, and ordei *Polygamia Frustanea;* the Marigold of the same class, but of the order *Polygamia Necessaria;* and the Heli· otrope of the class *Pentandria*, and order *Monogynia*."

SUN-FLOWER, &c.

As the Sun-flower turns to her god, when he sets,
The same look which she turn'd when he rose.

MOORE.

And Sun-flowers planting, for their gilded show,
That scale the window's lattice ere they blow,
Then, sweet to habitants within the sheds,
Peep through the diamond panes their golden heads.

CLARE.

What yellow, lovely as the golden morn,
The Eupine and the Heliotrope adorn!

ANON

THE HELIOTROPE

ANON.

There is a flower, whose modest eye
   Is turn'd with looks of light and love,
Who breathes her softest, sweetest sigh,
   Whene'er the sun is bright above.

Let clouds obscure, or darkness veil
　　Her fond idolatry is fled;
Her sighs no more their sweets exhale,—
　　The loving eye is cold and dead

Canst thou not trace a moral here,
　　False flatterer of the prosperous hour?
Let but an adverse cloud appear,
　　And thou art faithless as the flower!

———

THE MARIGOLD.

ANON.

THE Marigold, that goes to bed with the sun,
And with him rises weeping.

The same.—WITHER.

WHEN with a serious musing I behold
The grateful and obsequious Marigold,—
How duly, every morning, she displays
Her open breast when Phœbus spreads his rays;
How she observes him in his daily walk,
Still bending tow'rds him her small slender stalk;
How, when he down declines, she droops and mourns
Bedew'd, as 't were with tears, till he returns;
And how she veils her flowers when he is gone.
As if she scorned to be look'd upon

By an inferior eye, or did contemn
To wait upon a meaner light than him:
When this I meditate, methinks the flowers
Have spirits far more generous than ours,
And give us fair examples, to despise
The servile fawnings and idolatries
Wherewith we count these earthly things below,
Which merit not the service we bestow;
But, O my God! though grovelling I appear
Upon the ground, and have a rooting here
Which hales me downward, yet in my desire
To that which is above me I aspire:
And all my best affections I profess
To him that is the Sun of Righteousness.
Oh! keep the morning of his incarnation,
The burning noontide of his bitter passion,
The night of his descending, and the height
Of his ascension, ever in my sight;
That, imitating him in what I may,
I never follow an inferior way.

14*

THE AMARANTH.

The Amaranth, which is also called Flower-gentle, and Velvet-flower, derives its botanical name from a Greek word which signifies unfading.

Among the many species of Amaranth, the most beautiful is the Tree Amaranth, and the long pendulous Amaranth with reddish-coloured seeds, commonly called *Love lies a bleeding.* The origin of this name has not yet been discovered.

Of the Globe Amaranth there are several varieties — white, purple, striped, &c. The purple resembles clover raised to an intense pitch of colour, and sprinkled with grains of gold. The flowers, gathered when full grown, hung in the shade, will preserve their beauty for years, particularly if they are not exposed to the sun. In Portugal and other warm countries, the churches are in winter adorned with the Globe Amaranth.

———

By the streams that ever flow,
By the fragrant winds that blow
  O'er the Elysian flowers;
By the fragrant winds that dwell
In yellow meads of Asphodel,
  Or amaranthine bowers.

              POPE.

POETICAL AMARANTH.

Milton.

IMMORTAL Amaranth, a flower which once
In Paradise, fast by the tree of life,
Began to bloom, but soon for man's offence
To heaven removed, where first it grew, there grows
And flowers aloft, shading the fount of life
And where the river of bliss through midst of heaven
Rolls o'er Elysian flowers her amber stream;
With these, that never fade, the spirits elect
Bind their resplendent locks, enwreathed with beams;
Now in loose garlands, thick thrown off, the bright
Pavement, that like a sea of jasper shone,
Impurpled with celestial Roses, smiled.

TO THE WILD AMARANTH.

ANON.

THE *Rose*, that gave its perfume to the gale,
And triumph'd for an hour, in gay parade
Pride of Damascus, bright imperial flower,
    Was born to fade!
Shorn of its bloom, and rifled of its power,
Scared by the blast, and scatter'd in the vale!

So youth shall wither, beauty pass away!
The bloom of health, the flush of mantling pride,
Nor wealth, nor skill, nor eloquence, can save

From swift decay!
Beauty and youth are dust to dust allied,
And time returns its tribute to the grave!

Pale, unobtrusive tenant of the field!
Thy fair, unsullied form shall still remain,
'Mid summer's heat and autumn's chill career
  And winter's reign;
E'en the first honours of the floral year
To thee alone shall gay Narcissus yield.

Fair emblem art thou of the pious breast!
Like thee, unfading flower, shall virtue bloom
When youth and all its bustling pride repose
  Deep in the tomb!
When beauty's cheek shall wither like the Rose,
And beauty's sparkling eye shall be at rest!

THE ALOE.

THE aloe is made the emblem of acute sorrow, on ac
count of its painful bitterness.   The bitter of the aloe
affects the body, that of affliction reaches the soul.

———

SORROW that locks up the struggling heart.

AKENSIDE.

IF you do sorrow at my grief in love
By giving love your sorrow and my grief
Were both extermined.

SHAKSPEARE.

BESIDES, you know,
Prosperity's the very bond of love;
Whose fresh complexion, and whose heart together
Affliction alters.

WINTER'S TALE.

(155)

THE WHITE JASMINE.

THE beauty of this unassuming flower is even surpassed
by its delightful odour; may we thus always find loveliness accompanied by amiability!

AND brides, as delicate and fair
As the white jasmine flowers they wear.

T. MOORE.

THE jessamine, with which the queen of flowers
To charm her god, adorns his favourite bowers;
Which brides by the plain hand of neatness drest,
Unenvied rival! wear upon their breast;
Sweet as the incense of the morn, and chaste
As the pure zone which circles Dian's waist.

CHURCHILL

THE VIRGIN'S-BOWER.

WHEN artifice is innocently resorted to for the purpose
of giving pleasure, it may be compared to the agreeable
fragrance of the sweet clematis. But when it is used to
entangle the unwary, it becomes the agent of him whom
Milton thus describes;

He, soon aware,
Each perturbation smooth'd with outward calm,
Artificer of fraud! and was the first
That practised falsehood under saintly show.

Clematis, wreath afresh thy garden bower.

And virgin's bower, trailing airily.

KEATS.

THE LAVENDER.

In the floral emblems of the Turks, this agreeable plant represents assiduity; but the continental emblematists make it symbolical of mistrust and disunion, because it is frequently used to cover disagreeable odours.

Mistrust can only belong justly to such as are accustomed to cheat and deceive, and those need no greater curse for their misdeeds.

And lavender, whose spikes of azure bloom
Shall be erewhile in arid bundles bound,
To lurk amidst her labours of the loom,
And crown her kerchiefs clean with mickle rare perfume.

SHENSTONE.

THE PIMPERNEL.

THIS sensitive little flower is made the symbol of as signation, because the closing of its petals foretels wet; but when fully expanded it proclaims fair and dry weather. It is consequently called the peasant's barometer, and the shepherd's weather-glass.

The peasant loiters at the appointed stile, and the

> —————————— " Shepherd tells his tale
> Under the hawthorn in the dale."
>
> MILTON.

CLOSED is the pink-ey'd pimpernel.

*   *   *   *   *

'T will surely rain, I see, with sorrow.
Our jaunt must be put off to-morrow."

> DR. JENNER.

THE SENSITIVE PLANT.

MODESTY becomes the brave as well as the fair. Young says,

> Of boasting more than of a tomb afraid;
> A soldier should be modest as a maid.

WHENCE does it happen that the plant, which well
We name sensitive, should move and feel?
When know her leaves to answer her command,
And with quick horror fly the neighbouring hand?

PRIOR'S SOLOMON.

THIS little plant — how cautiously it meets
Th' approaching hand! advance, and it retreats!
See how it flies from the supposed disgrace,
And shrinks from contact of the rude embrace!

So wisdom folly should for ever shun;
So virtue from the touch of vice should run;
So female beauty should from flatt'ry fly,
And spurn the incense of the gilded lie.

THE HONEYSUCKLE, OR WOODBINE.

So doth the woodbine, the sweet honeysuckle
Gently entwine.

THIS happy emblem reminds us that sweetness of disposition is a firmer tie thar dazzling beauty.

COPIOUS of flowers, the woodbine, pale and wan,
But well compensating her sickly looks
With never-cloying odours, early and late.

COWPER.

ORANGE FLOWERS.

THESE fragrant blossoms are made the emblem of chastity from the purity of their white petals.   One of the principal beauties of the orange tree consists in its bearing fruit and flowers at the same time, as is beautifully noticed by Pope:

Here orange trees with blossoms and pendants shine,
And vernal honours to their autumn join;
Exceed their promise in the ripen'd store,
Yet in the rising blossom promise more.

THE punic granate op'd its rose-like flowers,
The orange breathed its aromatic powers.

SWIFT.

BUTTER-CUPS.

THIS flower, which so gaily bedecks our meadows with its golden petals, and enters so frequently into the sports of infancy, is presented as a meet emblem of childishness.

AND daisy there, and cowslip too,
And butter-cups of golden hue,
The children meet as soon as sought,
And gain their wish as soon as thought;
Who oft, I ween, the children's way,
Will leap the threshold's bounds to play.

VILLAGE MINSTREL

THE POPPY.

In floral language, the poppy is made the symbol of consolation to the sick, since it procures ease and sleep to the restless invalid.

Fertility was hieroglyphically described by Venus, with a head of poppy in her hand.

And poppies, which bind fast escaping sleep.

COLUMELLA.

From the Poppy I have ta'en
Mortals balm, and mortals bane!
Juice, that creeping through the heart,
Deadens every sense of smart.

MRS. M. ROBINSON.

THE STINGING NETTLE.

The nettle carries its cruel venom in a bag at the base of the sting, always ready to perforate the incautious, and throw in its vegetable poison, which, like slander, attacks even the brave when it can act slyly. But, neither the sting of the nettle, nor the tooth of a viper, is so much to be dreaded as the tongue of a slanderer.

AND rampant nettles lift the spiry head.

BLOOMFIELD.

SOME so like to thorns and nettles live,
That none for them can, when they perish, grieve.

WALLER

THE RHODODENDRON.

THESE purple flowers abound in a poisonous honey, and have hence been made emblematical of the dangers that lurk about the imperial purple.

O'ER pine-clad hills, and dusky plains,
In silent state rhodendron reigns,
And spreads, in beauty's softest blooms,
Her purple glories through the glooms.

SHAW.

Ev'n as those bees of Trebizond, —
  Which from the sunniest flowers that clad
With their pure smile the garden round,
  Draw venom forth that drives men mad.

T. MOORE

THE CYPRESS TREE.

THIS tree has been dedicated to sorrow and death in all civilized countries, and in all ages from the destruction of Troy to the present day.

THE mournful cypress rises round,
Tap'ring from the burial ground.

LUCAN.

IN mournful pomp the matrons walk the round,
With baleful cypress and blue fillets crown'd,
With eyes dejected, and with hair unbound.

ÆNEAS, Book 3

THE BLUE-BOTTLE CENTAURY.

THIS beautiful corn flower, the subject of the following verses, is made the emblem of delicacy from the purity of its celestial colour, which is not equal'ed by the fines ultramarine, and scarcely surpassed by the azure veins of youthful beauty.

THERE is a flower, a purple flower
Sown by the wind, nursed by the shower,

15*

O'er which Love has breathed a power and spell
The truth of whispering hope to tell.

*   *   *   *   *   *

And with scarlet poppies around like a bower,
Found the maiden her mystic flower.
Now, gentle flower, I pray thee tell
If my lover loves me, and loves me well;
So may the fall of the morning dew
Keep the sun from fading thy tender blue.

L. E. L.

THE SWEET-PEA.

FROM the charms this flower displays both in fragrance
and colour it has become the emblem of *Delicate Pleasure.*

THESE delicacies,
I mean of taste, sight, smell, herbs, fruit, and flowers.

MILTON.

HERE are sweet-peas on tip-toe for a flight,
The wings of gentle flush, o'er delicate white,
And taper fingers catching at all things
To bind them all about with tiny rings.

KEATS.

THE MEZEREON.

ɪɴ floral language, this early flowering shrub is made
to express a desire to please, whilst others make it one
of the emblems of coquetry, comparing it to a nymph,
who in the midst of winter seeks admiration in her summer robes.

LEAVE such to trifle with more grace and ease,
Whom folly pleases, and whose follies please.

POPE.

MEZEREON too,
Though leafless, well attired, and thick beset
With blushing wreaths, investing every spray.

COWPER.

THE NARCISSUS.

FROM Ovid's beautiful metamorphosis of the lovely and
coy Narcissus into this flower it has become the emblem
of Egotism and Self-Love.

NARCISSUS on the grassy verdure lies :
But whilst within the crystal fount he tries
To quench his heat, he feels new heats arise.

For as his own bright image he survey'd,
He fell in love with the fantastic shade;
And o'er the fair resemblance hung unmoved:
Nor knew, fond youth! it was himself he loved.

NARCISSUS fair,
As o'er the fabled fountain hanging still. *

THOMSON.

THE CONVOLVULUS MAJOR.

THIS flower is given to the ladies, that when they have
made their happy choice, they may have an appropriate
flower to bestow on their hopeless suitors, so as to extinguish the flame their charms have created. It is the emblem of extinguished hopes.

CONVOLVULUS, expand thy cup-like flower,
Graceful in form, and beautiful in hue.

THE soft god of pleasures that warm'd our desires,
Has broken his bow, and extinguish'd his fires.

DRYDEN.

THE ROSEMARY.

Rosemary was formerly worn at weddings, to signify the fidelity of the lovers. It was also an emblem of re-membrance.

I meet few but are stuck with rosemary: every one asked me who was to be married.

NOBLE SPANISH SOLDIER.

There's rosemary for you, that's for remembrance; pray you love, remember.

OPHELIA.

He, from his lass him lavender has sent,
Showing her love, and doth requital crave;
Him rosemary his sweetheart, whose intent
Is that he her should in remembrance have.

DRAYTON.

THE IVY.

This emblem of generous friendship attaches itself to the wretched.

As the ivy, when blasts howl before it,
  Clasps the bough it encircles more tight;
So my heart, in the storms that break o'er it,
  More closely to thine shall unite.

Then com? to this bosom — 'tis bleeding and bare,
But the child of affliction may find a home there.

W. W. B

I LOVE the ivy-mantled tower,
Rock'd by the storm of thousand years.

CUNNINGHAM

THUS stands an aged elm, in ivy bound,
Thus youthful ivy clasps an elm around.

PARNELL.

THE YELLOW IRIS.

THIS flag flower is made to represent —

My heart's on flame, and does like fire
To her aspire.

COWLEY.

No warning of th' approaching time,
Swiftly like sudden death it came —
I loved the moment I beheld.

GRANVILLE.

AMID its waving swords, in flowing gold
The Iris towers —————.

MRS. C SMITH

THE COLUMBINE.

THIS flower is made the emblem of folly, either on account of its party-coloured corolla, or in allusion to the
shape of its nectary, which turns over like the cap of the
old jesters.

—————————————— AND entwine
The white, the blue, the flesh-like columbine.

W. BROWNE.

THE columbine in tawny often taken,
Is then ascribed to such as are forsaken.

IBID.

THE ALMOND.

THE blushing petals which bedeck the leafless branches
of these trees that of old embellished the banks of the Jor-
dan, are made emblematical of heedlessness, from their
venturing forth before nature has prepared the foliage for
their protection.

LIKE to an almond-tree, mounted high
On top of green Selenis, all alone,
With blossoms brave bedecked daintily;
Whose tender locks do tremble every one,
At every little breath that under heaven is blown.

FAERY QUEEN

16

MARK well the flow'ring almonds in the wood:
If od'rous blossoms the bearing branches load,
The glebe will answer to the sylvan reign,
Great heats will follow, and large crops of grain.

                                    DRYDEN.

BROOM.

Even humble broom and osiers have their use.

IN the hieroglyphical language of flowers, the broom is made the emblem of Humility from the following historical anecdote.

Fulke, Earl of Anjou, having been guilty of some crime, was enjoined, by way of penance, to go to the Holy Land and submit to castigation. He acquiesced, habited himself in lowly attire, and, as a mark of his humility, wore a sprig of broom in his cap.

The expiation being happily finished, Fulke adopted the name of Plantagenet, from the Latin of this shrub, planta-genesta.

His descendants continued the name, and many successive nobles of the line of Anjou, distinguished themselves by decorating their helmets with this plant.

The arms of Richard the First were, "two lions combat-ant." Crest, a plantagenista, or broom sprig. Upon his great seal, a broom sprig is placed on each side of his throne. — *Sandford's Genealogical History.*

———————— the broom,
Yellow and bright as bullion unalloy'd,
Her blossoms.

THE COMMON THISTLE.

THIS plant, that furnishes its seeds with wings by which
it flies from hill to dale, too frequently intrudes itself into
our fields, to the injury of the farmer's best hopes. It is
therefore made the emblem of Importunity.

Now where the thistle blows his feather'd seed,
Which frolic zephyrs buffet in the air.

FALCONER.

WIDE o'er the thistly lawn as swells the breeze,
A whitening shower of vegetable down
Amusive floats.

THOMSON.

TOUGH thistles chok'd the fields, and kill'd the corn,
And an unthrifty crop of weeds was born.

DRYDEN.

THE ASPEN TREE.

BIGOTED ignorance states that the cross was made from
this tree, since which time the leaves have never known
rest, and from hence the emblem seems to have originated

Why tremble so, broad aspen tree!
Why shake thy leaves, ne'er ceasing?
At rest thou never seem'st to be,
For when the air is still and clear,
Or when the nipping gale increasing,
Shakes from thy boughs soft twilight's tear,
Thou tremblest still, broad aspen tree,
And never tranquil seem'st to be.

ANON.

.

THE STOCK, OR GILLYFLOWER.

LASTING beauty is represented by this flower whose charms, although less graceful than the rose or the lily, are more durable, and consequently embellish the parterre for a greater length of time.

FAIR is the gillyflower of gardens sweet.

GAY.

AND lavish stock, that scents the garden round.

THOMSON

Herbs and flowers, the beauteous birth
Of the genial womb of earth,
Suffer but a transient death,
From the winter's cruel breath!

Zephyr speaks — serener skies,
Warm the glebe, and they arise!
We, alas! earth's haughty kings,
We that promise mighty things,
Losing soon life's happy prime,
Droop and fade in little time,
Spring returns, but not our bloom
Still 't is winter in the tomb!

COWPER.

THE MYRTLE.

MYTHOLOGICAL writers state that when Venus first sprang from the bosom of the waves, the Hours preceded her with a garland of myrtle, since which it has been dedicated to the goddess of beauty, and made the emblem of love.

THE lover's myrtle.

THOMSON.

Like a myrtle tree in flower
Taken from an Asian bower,
Where with many a dewy cup,
Nymphs in play had nursed it up.

HUNT'S CATULLUS.

THE lover with the myrtle sprays
Adorns his crisped tresses.

DRAYTON.

16*

IMPERIAL passion! sacred fire!

When we of meaner subjects sing,

Thou tun'st our harp, thou dost our souls inspire;

'T is love directs the quill, 't is love strikes every string

ANON

Love! that vast passion of the mind,

 Whose roving flame does traverse o'er

 All nature's good, and search for more;

Still to thy magic spheres confined,

 'T is beauty's all we can desire;

 Beauty the native mansion of love's fire.

THE CROWN IMPERIAL.

THIS Persian flower, that towers above the more humble plants of the parterre, holds a high rank in floral
emblems.

The crown imperial; lilies of all kinds,

The fleur-de-luce being one! O, these I lack,

To make you garlands of.

· SHAKSPEARE.

THE lily's height bespake command,

 A fair imperial flower;

She seem'd design'd for Flora's hand,

 The sceptre of her power.

THE IRIS.

THIS flower, which the poets have chosen as the emblem of the messenger of the gods, takes its name from the celestial bow, on account of its various colours.

———

THE various iris, Juno sends with haste.

L'IRIS que flore a prise aux cieux.

NOR iris, with her glorious rainbow clothed
So fulgent, as the cheerful gardens shine
With their bright offspring.

———

THE DANDELION.

THE medicinal properties of this plant have caused it to be familiarly known by a name that has brought it into contempt, and on which account it is presumed the emblem originated. It is the emblem of an *Oracle*.

———

——————— DANDELION this,
A college youth, that flashes for a day
All gold; anon he doffs his gaudy suit,
Touch'd by the magic hand of some grave bishop,

And all at once, by commutation strange,
Becomes a reverend divine.

HURDIS.

Why, by the verities on thee made good,
May they not be my oracles.

SHAKSPEARE

THE MISTLETOE.

This plant, which is without an earthly inheritance,
makes no difficulty in attaching itself to the branches of
lofty trees, and there, without apparent labour, subsists
upon the ascending sap of its supporter.

When drawn suspended on a tree, it is the symbol of
a flattering hanger-on.

The naturalists are puzzled to explain
How trees did first this stranger entertain;
Whether the busy birds ingraft it there,
Or, else, some deity's mysterious care,
As Druids thought; for when the blasted oak
By lightning falls, this plant escapes the stroke.

GARTH.

THE OLIVE.

FROM the time of the general deluge to the present day the olive branch has ever been the emblem of peace.

BUT he her fears to cease,
Sent down the meek-ey'd Peace;
She, crown'd with olive green, came softly sliding
Down through the turning sphere,
His ready harbinger;
With turtle wing, the amorous clouds dividing,
And waving wide her myrtle wand,
She strikes an universal peace through sea and land.

THE STRAWBERRY.

THIS agreeable and wholesome fruit is made the symbol of perfect goodness, from its fragrance, flavour, and inoffensive qualities. Shakspeare says,

The strawberry grows underneath the nettle;
And wholesome berries thrive and ripen best,
Neighbour'd by fruit of baser quality.

CONTENT with food which nature freely bred
On wildings and strawberries they fed.

DRYDEN

THE MOUNTAIN ASH.

This elegant tree seems to have been selected as the emblem of prudence, from its foliage being withheld until the equinoctial winds have ceased to commit their devastations.

———

The mountain ash, whose flower-fill'd boughs
  Spread like a cloud at noon;
Whose shadow is a haunted place
  For the sweet airs of June.
    *   *   *   *   *   *
I wreathed amid thy hair
Its berries, like the coral crown
That the sea-maidens wear.

L. E. L.

THE CHESTNUT TREE.

This tree affords a wholesome nourishment to the inhabitants of many countries. It was of more importance in former days, and the roasting of these nuts is mentioned by poets whose verses will ever be admired, however time may change our customs.

———

New cheese and chestnuts are our country fare,
With mellow apples for your welcome cheer.

VIRGIL'S PASTORALS.

Or whose discourse with innocent delight
Shall fill me now, and cheat the wintry night?
While hisses on my hearth the pulpy pear,
And black'ning chestnuts start, and crackle there

MILTON.

A woman's tongue,
That gives not half so great a blow to th' ear,
As will a chestnut in a farmer's fire.

SHAKSPEARE.

LILY OF THE VALLEY.

This flower, whose odour is as agreeable as its form is elegant, announces the happy season of May, when

———————— new verdure clothes the plain,
And earth assumes her transient youth again.

MILTON.

——————— And ye, whose lowlier pride
In sweet seclusion seems to shrink from view,—
You of the valley named, no longer hide
Your blossoms meet to twine the brow of purest bride.

BARTON.

Then the sweet lily of the vale
In woodland dells is found,
While whisp'ring winds its sweets exhale
And waft its fragrance round.

LOTUS FLOWER, OR WATER LILY

WHERE blameless pleasures dimple quiet's cheek,
As water-lilies ripple a slow stream!

COLERIDGE.

WE present this aquatic plant as the emblem of silence since the antiquarians assure us, that they recognize this flower on the head of Harpocrates.

Love glides silently upon us, and the Indians feign that Cupid was first seen floating down the Ganges on the *Nymphæa Nelumbo.*

> Down the blue Ganges laughing glide
> Upon a rosy lotus wreath,
> Catching new lustre from the tide,
> That with his image shone beneath.

T. MOORE.

The lotus is an object of supreme veneration in all the mythological systems of the east, especially in that of the Hindoos.

The sacred name of this plant is Pedma, and it is pretended that Brahma was born in a lotus, when he created the world, wherefore it is regarded as the symbol of creative power.

> And thy own pedma, roseate flower of light,
> Emblem and cradle of creative might.

C. GRANT.

This plant, (says Mr. Knight,) being productive of itself, and vegetating from its own matrice, without being fostered in the earth, was naturally adopted as the symbol of the productive power of waters, upon which the active spirit of the creator operated, in giving life and vegetation to matter

---

DRAGON PLANT.

Oh! wander not where dragon Arum showers
Her baleful dews, and twines her purple flowers,
Lest round thy neck she throw her snaring arms,
Sap thy life's blood, and riot on thy charms.
Her shining berry, as the ruby bright,
Might please thy taste, and tempt thy eager sight:
Trust not this specious veil; beneath its guise,
In honey'd streams, a fatal poison lies.

MRS. F. A. ROWDEN.

The above lines were penned to caution children against the dangers of this beautiful vegetable production. But as children of a full growth are frequently entangled, we shall caution them in the words of Dryden, who says,

The spreading snare for all mankind is laid,
And lovers all betray or are betray'd.

17

THE HEATH.

THE beautiful heath with its purple bells, has been chosen for the emblem of solitude, because it grows only in a barren soil, and consequently in dreary situations.

————

WHAT call'st thou solitude? Is not the earth
With various living creatures, and the air,
Replenish'd, and all these at thy command,
To come and play before thee?

MILTON.

——— THE Erica here,
That o'er the Caledonian hills sublime,
Spreads its dark mantle, (where the bees delight
To seek their purest honey,) flourishes.

MRS. C. SMITH

To you, ye wastes, whose artless charms
   Ne'er drew ambition's eye,
'Scap'd a tumultuous world's alarms,
   To your retreats I fly.

Deep in your most sequester'd bower,
   Let me at last recline;
Where solitude, mild modest power,
   Leans on her ivy'd shrine.

BEATTIE

THE ADONIS.

FABLE tells us that Adonis stained with his blood the flower that bears his name, and hence it has been made the emblem of sorrowful remembrances.

Some poets make this flower symbolical of the chase, in allusion to Adonis's love of hunting.

———

THEN on the blood sweet nectar she bestows,
The scented blood in little bubbles rose:
Little as falling drops, which flutt'ring fly,
Borne by the winds along a low'ring sky.
Short time ensued, till where the blood was shed,
A flow'r began to rear its purple head.

EUSDEN'S OVID.

ON the discolour'd grass Adonis lay,
The monster trampling o'er his beauteous prey
     *   *   *   *
Yet dares not Venus with a change surprise,
And in a flower bid her fall'n here rise.

17*

THE CEDAR TREE

THE use of this wood for all purposes requiring *strength*, has been proverbial from the time of Solomon to the present day.

————

YET heaven their various plants for use designs,
For houses, cedars; and for shipping, pines.

VIRGIL.

———— CEDARS here,
Coeval with the sky-crown'd mountain's self,
Spread wide their giant arms.

MASON.

THE WHITE PINK.

THIS flower, so richly gifted with odour, is emblematic of those persons who benefit society by their talents.

————

SWEET flower, beneath thy natal sky
   No fav'ring smiles thy scents invite;
To Britain's worthier regions fly,
   And paint her meadows with delight.

SHAW.

EACH pink sends forth its choicest sweet
Aurora's warm embrace to meet.

MRS. M. ROBINSON

MINT.

THE medicinal properties of this herb were formerly held in such high estimation, that the plant became the emblem of virtue.

VIRTUE only makes our bliss below.

POPE.

THEN rubb'd it o'er with newly-gather'd mint,
A wholesome herb, that breathed a grateful scent.

ANON.

LETTUCE.

IT is fabled, that after the death of Adonis, Venus laid upon a bed of lettuce.

FAT colworts, and comforting purseline,
Cold lettuce, and refreshing rosemarine.

SPENSER.

AND now let lettuce, with its healthful sleep,
Make haste, which of a tedious long disease
The painful loathings cures.

COLUMELLA.

LUPIN.

THE ancients named this plant *Lupinus*, from *Lupus*, a wolf, on account of its voracious nature, which is such that it draws in all the nourishment of the soil to feed its own growth, and consequently, destroys other vegetation; but in doing so it forms an excellent manure for poor and foul lands.

———

——— Tristisque lupini
Sustuleris fragiles calamos.

VIRGIL.

——— WHERE stalks of lupins grew,
Th' ensuing season, in return, may bear
'The bearded product of the golden year.

DRYDEN.

GUELDER-ROSE.

THIS cold-coloured, abortive flower is made to represent he age which banishes gaiety and warm desire

———

THE snow-ball which eclipses
The white bosom of Venus.

HER silver globes, light as the foamy surf
That the wind severs from the broken wave.

COWPER.

AFTER summer, evermore succeeds
The barren winter, with his nipping cold.

SHAKSPEARE.

AND on this forehead, (where your verse has said
The loves delighted, and the graces play'd,)
Insulting age will trace his cruel way,
And leave sad marks of his destructive sway.

PRIOR.

THE MULBERRY-TREE.

PLINY observes, that the mulberry-tree was esteemed the wisest of all the trees, because it never expanded its buds until all fear of frost was past, and hence the origin of the emblem, Wisdom.

———— THE green leaf
Which feeds the spinning worm.

AND that old mulberry that shades the court
Has been my joy from very childhood up.

H. KIRKE WHITE

PRONOUNCE him blest, my muse, whom wisdom guides
In her own path to her own heavenly seat;
Through all the storms his soul securely glides,
Nor can the tempest, nor the tides
That rise and roar around, supplant his steady feet.

WATTS.

THE FOX-GLOVE.

EXPLORE the fox-glove's freckled bell.

MRS. CHARLOTTE SMITH.

THE light down which covers the stalks of this plant,
induced the poets to make it the emblem of youth.

YOUTH, ah stay, prolong delight,
Close thy pinions stretch'd for flight;
Youth disdaining silver hairs,
Autumn's frowns, and winter's cares,
Dwell'st thou but in dimple sleek,
In vernal smiles, and summer's cheek?
On spring's ambrosial lap thy hands unfold,
They blossom fresh with hope, and all thy touch is gold

LOVIBOND.

THE ELDER.

This native tree, which forms the dispensary of the English peasantry, seems zealous in their service, for it is so tenacious of life, that it thrives not only in swampy grounds, wet ditches, arid and sterile banks, but it grows also on the ruins of old towers, and is frequently seen self-planted on the trunks of decaying trees.

There the favourite elder was planted,
Whose wide-extending branches shelter'd
The early plants of the rustic garden,
Whilst its umbels of faint-smelling flowers
Afforded them their only cosmetic,
And its purple berries their only wine.
Its first young buds form'd their only pickle;
Its pithy stalks their children's only toy.

THE LEMON.

This fragrant plant, whose fruit imparts such an agreeable relish to the board and the bowl, we present as the emblem of zest, and should our pages give a similar zest for a novel and innocent amusement, we shall deem our labours most pleasingly rewarded.

BEAR me, Pomona,
To where the lemon and the piercing lime,
With the deep orange, glowing through the green,
Their lighter glories blend.

NOR be the citron, Media's boast, unsung.

SHARP-TASTED citron Median climes produce,
Bitter the rind, but generous the juice;
A cordial fruit.

THE ACANTHUS.

THE Acanthus is found in hot countries, along the shores of great rivers.

It grows freely in our climate; and Pliny assures us that it is a garden herb, and is admirably adapted for ornament and embellishment. The ancients tastefully adorned their furniture, vases, and most costly attire, with its elegant leaves. And Virgil says, that the robe of Helen was bordered with a wreath of acanthus in relief.

This beautiful model of the arts has become their emblem; and he will be talented indeed, who shall produce any thing to excel its richness. If any obstacle resists the growth of the acanthus, it seems to struggle to overcome it, and to vegetate with renewed vigour. So genius, when acted upon by resistance or opposition, redoubles its attempts to overthrow every impediment.

It is said that the architect, Callimach, passing near the tomb of a young maiden who had died a few days before the time appointed for her nuptials, moved by tenderness and pity, approached to scatter some flowers on her tomb Another tribute to her memory had preceded his. Her nurse had collected the flowers which should have decked her on her wedding-day; and, putting them with the marriage veil, in a little basket, had placed it near the grave upon a plant of acanthus, and then covered it with a tile In the succeeding spring the leaves of the acanthus grew round the basket; but, being stayed in their growth by the projecting tile, they recoiled and surmounted its extremities. Callimach, surprised by this rural decoration, which seemed the work of the Graces in tears, conceived the capital of the Corinthian column, a magnificent ornament, still used and admired by the whole civilized world.

———

———— THE roof
Of thickest covert was inwoven shade;
Laurel and myrtle, and what higher grew
Of firm and fragrant leaf; on either side
Acanthus, and each odorous bushy shrub,
Fenced up the verdant wall; each beauteous flower,
Iris all hues, roses, and jessamine,
Rear'd high their flourish'd heads between, and wrought
Mosaic; underfoot the violet,
Crocus, and hyacinth, with rich inlay,
Broider'd the ground, more colour'd than with stone,
Of costliest emblem.

THE FIR-TREE.

THE fir-tree rears its head upon the loftiest mountains and in the coldest regions of the earth, without the aid of man. The resinous juices of this tree defy the rigorous frost to congeal its sap, while its filiform leaves are well adapted to resist the impetuous winds, which beat with violence on the lofty situations where fir-trees are found.

———

TOWERING firs in conic forms arise,
And with a pointed spear divide the skies.

PRIOR.

THE VERVAIN.

IT were well if botanists would attach a moral idea to every plant they describe; we might then have an universal dictionary of the Sentiment of Flowers — generally understood, — which would be handed down from age to age, and might be renewed, without changing their characters, every succeeding spring.

The altars of Jupiter are overthrown; those ancient forests, that witnessed the mysteries of Druidism, exist no longer; and the pyramids of Egypt shall one day disappear, buried like the sphinx, in the sands of the desert · but the lotus and the acanthus shall ever flower upon the banks of the Nile, the mistletoe will always flourish upon the oak, and the vervain upon the barren knolls.

Vervain was used by the ancients for divers kinds of divinations; they attributed to it a thousand properties, among others, that of reconciling enemies; and when the Roman heralds at arms were despatched with a message of peace or war to other nations, they wore a wreath of vervain.

The Druids held this plant in great veneration, and, before gathering it, they made a sacrifice to the earth. Probably they used it for food.

We are told that the worshippers of the sun, in performing their services, held branches of vervain in their hands. Venus Victorious wore a crown of myrtle interwoven with vervain, and the Germans to this day give a hat of vervain to the new married bride, as putting her under the protection of that goddess. Pliny also tells us that it was made use of by the Druids in casting lots. in drawing omens, and in other magical arts.

SHE night-shade strows to work him ill,
Therewith the vervain and her dill,
That hindereth witches of their will.

DRAYTON.

A WREATH of vervain heralds wear,
    Amongst our garlands named,
Being sent that dreadful news to bear,
    Offensive war proclaim'd.

DRAYTON.

SOME scattering pot-herbs here and there he found,
Which, cultivated with his daily care,
And bruised with vervain, were his daily fare.

DRYDEN.

THE LILAC.

THE lilac is consecrated to the first emotion of love because nothing is more delightful than the sensations it produces by its first appearance on the return of spring. The freshness of its verdure, the pliancy of its tender branches, the abundance of its flowers, — their beauty, though brief and transient, — their delicate and varied colours; — all their qualities summon up those sweet emotions which enrich beauty, and impart to youth a grace divine.

Albano was unable to blend, upon the palette which love had confided to him, colours sufficiently soft and delicate to convey the peculiarly beautiful tints which adorn the human face in early youth;

> The velvet down that spreads the cheek;

Van Spaendock himself laid down his pencil in despair before a bunch of lilac. Nature seems to have aimed to produce massy bunches of these flowers, every part of which should astonish by its delicacy and its variety. The gradation of colour, from the purple bud to the almost colourless flowers, is the least charm of these beautiful

groups, around wh.ch the light plays and produces a thou·
sand shades, which all blending together in the same tint,
forms that matchless harmony which the painter despairs
to imitate, and the most indifferent observer delights to
behold. What labour has Nature bestowed to create this
fragile shrub, which seems only given for the gratification
of the senses! What an union of perfume, of freshness,
of grace, and of delicacy! What variety in detail! What
beauty as a whole!

———————

THE lilac, various in array, now white,
Now sanguine, and her beauteous head now set
With purple spikes pyramidal, as if
Studious of ornament, yet unresolved
Which hue she most approved, she chose them all.

COWPER.

BEAUTY's rosy ray
In flying blushes richly play;
Blushes of that celestial flame
Which lights the cheek of virgin shame.

ANACREON.

———————

THE HOLLY.

IN that delightful work, Jesse's Gleanings in Natural
History, the eloquent author, speaking of the holly, says,
— "The economy of trees, plants, and vegetables, is a
curious subject of inquiry, and in all of them we may
18*

trace the hand of a beneficent Creato.; the same care which he has bestowed on his creatures is extended to plants; this is remarkably the case with respect to hollies: the edges of the leaves are provided with strong sharp spines, as high up as they are within the reach of cattle; above that height the leaves are generally smooth, the protecting spines being no longer necessary.

O READER! hast thou ever stood to see
The holly tree?
The eye that contemplates it well perceives
Its glossy leaves;
Order'd by an Intelligence so wise
As might confound an atheist's sophistries.

Below a circling fence, its leaves are seen
Wrinkled and keen;
No grazing cattle through their prickly round
Can reach to wound;
But, as they grow where nothing is to fear,
Smooth and unarm'd the pointless leaves appear.

SOUTHEY.

THE HYACINTH.

THE following address to the hyacinth is extracted from Tait's Magazine. The lines were sent to the editor of that excellent periodical as the production of a young country

girl in the north of Ireland. We agree with him in say-
ing (if that statement be true), that they are indeed more
. than wonderful. They refer to the fate of Hyacinthus,
who was killed by a quoit while playing at that game
with Apollo.

Oh! mournful, graceful, sapphire-coloured flower,
   That keep'st thine eye for ever fix'd on earth!
   Gentle and sad, a foe thou seem'st to mirth—
What secret sorrow makes thee thus to lower?

Perhaps 'tis that thy place thou canst not change,
   And thou art pining at thy prison'd lot;
   But oh! where couldst thou find a sweeter spot,
Wert thou permitted earth's wide bounds to range?

In pensive grove, meet temple for thy form,
   Where, with her silvery music, doth intrude
   The lucid stream, where nought unkind or rude
Durst break of harmony the hallow'd charm,

Thy beauties, all unseen by vulgar eyes,
   Sol, in his brightness, still delights to view;
   He clothes thy petals in his glorious hue,
To show how much of old he did thee prize.

And what the sighing zephyr hither brings,
   To wander in these muse-beloved dells—
   It is to linger 'midst thy drooping bells
While vain repentance in thine ear he sings.

And, sweetest flowel methinks thou hast forgiven
   Him who unconsciously did cause thy death;
   For, soon as thou hadst yielded up thy breath,
With grief for thee his frantic soul was riven.

And thou wert placed where mingle wave and breeze
   Their dreamy music with the vocal choir,
   Whose varied harmonies might seem a lyre,
Striving with dying notes thy soul to please—

Where winter ne'er ungraciously presumes
   To touch thee with his sacrilegious hand—
   Where thy meek handmaids are the dews so bland—
Where Spring around thee spreads her choicest blooms.

'Tis not revenge nor pining wretchedness,
   Thy head in pensive attitude that throws—
   'Tis extreme sensibility, that shows
In gesture, gratitude speech can't express.

E'en while I pay this tributary praise,
   Methinks a deeper tinge thy cheek doth flush;
   What, lovely one, need make thee thus to blush
And turn away from my enraptured gaze!

No, gentle Hyacinth, thou canst not grieve,
   When things so lovely worship in thy train—
   The sun, the wind, the wave—Oh! it were vain
To sum the homage which thou dost receive.

The sad and musing poetess you cheer—
At sight of thee Mem'ry's electric wings
Waft to her soul long, long forgotten things—
Loved voices hush'd in death she seems to hear.

ANON.

THE LAUREL.

THE Greeks and Romans consecrated crowns of laurel to glory of every kind. With them they adorned the brows of warriors and of poets, of orators and philosophers, of the vestal virgin and the emperor.

This beautiful shrub is found in abundance in the island of Delphos, where it grows naturally on the banks of the river Peneus. There, its aromatic and evergreen foliage is borne up by its aspiring branches to the height of the loftiest trees; and it is alleged that by a secret and peculiar power they avert the thunderbolt from the shores they beautify. The beautiful Daphne was the daughter of the river Peneus. She was beloved by Apollo; but, preferring virtue to the love of the most eloquent of gods, she fled, fearing that the eloquence of his speech should lead her from the paths of virtue. Apollo pursued her; and as he caught her, the nymph invoked the aid of her father, and was changed into the laurel.

In our free land, where letters are so extensively cultivated, they who succeed in exciting popular favour meet

with more remuneration than in ancient days; but how few
have been honoured so highly as their merits demand,
until the last debt of nature has been paid, and then the
marble bust, wreathed with bay, is raised to immortalize
his fame, when his ears are become deaf to praise. He
seldom receives his honours due while he enjoys the beauties of this terrestrial globe.

THE bard his glory ne'er receives,
  Where summer's common flowers are seen,
But winter finds it, when she leaves
  The laurel only green;
And Time, from that eternal tree,
Shall weave a wreath to honour thee.

CLARE.

THE FLAX-FLOWER.

THE utility of this plant and its connection with every
kind of adornment in apparel, from the earliest ages of
the world, richly entitle it to a place in the "Poetry o'
Flowers." Mary Howitt thus celebrates its praises,—

Oh, THE little flax-flower,
  It groweth on the hill,
And, be the breeze awake or sleep,
  It never standeth still.

It groweth, and it groweth fast;
    One day it is a seed,
And then a little grassy blade,
    Scarce better than a weed.
But then out comes the flax-flower,
    As blue as is the sky;
And "'t is a dainty little thing!"
    We say, as we go by.

An, 't is a goodly little ·thing,
    It groweth for the poor,
And many a peasant blesses it,
    Beside his cottage-door.
He thinketh how those slender stems
    That shimmer in the sun,
Are rich for him in web and woof,
    And shortly shall be spun.
He thinketh how those tender flowers,
    Of seed will yield him store;
And sees in thought his next-year's crop
    Blue shining round his door.

Oh, the little flax-flower!
    The mother, then says she,
" Go pull the thyme, the heath, the fern
    But let the flax-flower be !
It groweth for the children's sake,
    It groweth for our own;
There are flowers enough upon the hill.
    But leave the flax alone !

The farmer hath his fields of wheat,
　　Much cometh to his share;
We have this little plot of flax,
　　That we have tilled with care.

"Our squire he hath the holt and hil.,
　　Great halls and noble rent;
We only have the flax-field,
　　Yet therewith are content.
We watch it morn, we watch it night
　　And when the stars are out,
The good man and the little ones,
　　They pace it round about;
For it we wish the sun to shine,
　　For it the rain to fall;
Good lack! for who is poor doth make
　　Great count of what is small!"

Oh, the goodly flax-flower!
　　It groweth on the hill,
And, be the breeze awake or sleep,
　　It never standeth still!
It seemeth all astir with life,
　　As if it loved to thrive;
As if it had a merry heart
　　Within its stem alive!
Then fair befall the flax-field,
　　And may the kindly showers,
Give strength unto its shining stem,
　　Give seed unto its flowers!

PERUVIAN HELIOTROPE.

Tiis evergreen trailer is a native of Peru, and bears
beautiful lilac-coloured flowers; and, in the greenhouse, con·
tinues in bloom nearly the whole of the year.

The Orientals say that the perfumes of the heliotrope
elevate their souls towards heaven; it is true that they ex-
hilarate us, and produce a degree of intoxication. The sen·
sation produced by inhaling them, may, it is said, be renewed by imagination, even though years have passed away
after the reality was experienced.

The Countess Eleanora, natural daughter of Christian IV.,
king of Denmark, who became so notorious by the misfortunes, crimes, and exile of Count Ulfeld, her husband, offers
to us a striking proof of the power of perfumes on the
memory. This princess, at the age of thirteen, had become
attached to a young man to whom she was subsequently affianced. This young man died in the castle where they
were making preparations for the marriage. Elenora, in
despair, wished to take a long last look at the object of her
love; and, if alive, to bid a last adieu. She was conducted
into the chamber where he had just expired. The body was
already placed on a bier, and covered with rosemary. The
spectacle made such a deep impression upon the affianced
maiden, that though she afterwards exhibited courage equal
to her misfortunes, she never could breathe the perfume of
rosemary without falling into the most frightful convulsions.

The celebrated Jussieu, while botanising in the Cordilleras

suddenly inhaled the most exquisite perfumes. He expect
ed to find some brilliantly coloured flowers, but only per-
ceived some pretty clumps of an agreeable green, bearing
flowers of a pale blue colour. On approaching nearer, he
observed that the flowers turned gently towards the sun,
which they appeared to regard with reverential love. Struck
with this peculiar disposition, he gave the plant the name
of heliotrope, which is derived from two Greek words, sig-
nifying "sun," and "I turn." The learned botanist, delighted with this charming acquisition, collected a quantity
of the seeds, and sent them to the Jardin du Roi, at Paris,
where it was first cultivated in Europe. The ladies collected it with enthusiasm,—placed it in their richest vases,
—called it the flower of love,—and received with indifference every bouquet in which their favourite flower was
not to be found.

An anonymous writer has made it emblematical of flattery, as it is said that when a cloud obscures the sky, it
droops its head. We would rather suppose that, like the
lover, whose heart is sad when absent from his mistress,
so the heliotrope droops because it is deprived of the cheering rays of the sun that it seems to adore.

———

THERE is a flower whose modest eye
Is turn'd with looks of light and love,
Who breathes her softest, sweetest sigh,
Whene'er the sun is bright above.

Let clouds obscure, or darkness veil,
Her fond idolatry is fled;
Her sighs no more their sweets exhale,—
The loving eye is cold and dead.

Canst thou not trace a moral here,
False flatterer of the prosperous hour?
Let but an adverse cloud appear,
And thou art faithless as the flower!

THE VINE.

THE grateful juice of the-vine has been given to cheer
the heart of man; and though, alas! it is too often used
as the excitement to unseemly revelry, where men degrade
themselves to the condition of the brutes, over which they
were created lords, we confess we like to see

Depending vines the shelving caverns screen,
With purple clusters blushing through the green.

POPE.

But oh! let vines luxuriant roll
Their blushing tendrils round the bowl.

ANACREON

THE WHITE DAISY.

In the by-gone days of chivalry, when a lady wished to intimate to her lover that she was undecided whether sne would accept his offer or not, she decorated her head with a frontlet of white daisies, which was understood to say, "I will think of it."

An unknown poet has sung the daisy's offering in verses so agreeable to our ears that we must even let our readers share the pleasure.

> Think of the flowers cull'd for thee,
>   In vest of silvery white,
> When other flowers perchance you see,
>   Not fairer, but more bright.

> Sweet roses and carnations gay,
>   Have but a summer's reign;
> I mingle with the buds of May,
>   Join drear December's train.

> A simple unassuming flower,
>   'Mid showers and storms I bloom
> I'll decorate thy lady's bower,
>   And blossom on thy tomb.

THE WEEPING WILLOW

By the waters of Babylon we sat down and wept, when we remembered thee, O Sion! As for our harps we hanged them up
upon the willows that are therein.   PSALMS.

WE cannot conceive a more touching appeal to human
sympathy, than the mournful complaints of the daughters
of Jerusalem. Their Babylonish conquerors having led
them away captive, required of them "a song, and melody
in their heaviness; 'Sing us one of the songs of Sion.'"
But the hearts of her children were surcharged with grief,
and they asked, "How shall we sing the Lord's song in
a strange land?" They were oppressed with sorrow, —
they were bowed down with affliction, — they "hanged
their harps upon the willows, and sat down and wept."
Is not then the weeping willow a sacred emblem of melancholy?

The weeping willow is a native of the east, and is greatly
admired for its drooping pendulous branches, waving over
our lakes and streams.

It grows wild on the coast of Persia, and is common
in China. The celebrated specimen in Pope's garden at
Twickenham, is said to have been the first introduced into
England; but this we believe to be erroneous. The poet
chanced to be present on the opening of a package which
came from Spain, and observing that the sticks had some
vegetation, fancied they might produce something which
did not usually grow in England. With this idea he planted

a cutting, from whence sprang the parent tree of many
of the finest and most admired specimens.

My gentle harp! once more I waken
  The sweetness of thy slumbering strain;
In tears our last farewell was taken,
  And now in tears we meet again.

No light of joy hath o'er thee broken,
  But — like those harps, whose heav'nly skill
Of slavery, dark as thine, hath spoken —
  Thou hang'st upon the willows still.

ANON.

Thus o'er our streams do eastern willows lean
In pensive guise; whose grief-inspiring shade
Love has to melancholy sacred made.

DELILLE.

THE SORROWFUL GERANIUM.

This charming geranium, like a melancholy spirit, shuns
the light of day; but it enchants those who cultivate it by
the delightful perfumes it exhales. Its appearance is som-
bre, though unaffected; and, altogether, it forms a striking
contrast to the scarlet geranium, which is the emblem of
stupidity.

Few know that elegance of soul refined
Whose soft sensation feels a quicker joy
From melancholy's scenes, than the dull pride
Of tasteless splendour and magnificence
Can e'er afford.

WARTON

THE WHITE POPPY.

An insipid oil is expressed from the grains of the white poppy, which calms the senses and provokes sleep. Would not the unhappy lover, who dreads that the object of his love has no reciprocal feeling, thus express himself in the words of H. Smith?—

> O gentle sleep!
> Scatter thy drowsiest poppies from above;
> And in new dreams, not soon to vanish, bless
> My senses

Yea, gladly would he become insensible to the agonies of unrequited love

The palace of Somnus, who presided over sleep, was represented as a dark cave, into which the sun's rays never penetrated; and at the entrance grew poppies and other somniferous herbs; the Dreams watched over his couch, attended by Morpheus, his prime minister, holding a vase in one hand, and grasping poppies in the other.

THERL poppies white, and violet.
Alcippus on the altar sets
Of quiet sleep ; and weaves a crown
To bring the gentle godhead down.

FRACASTORO.

THE PHEASANT'S EYE ; OR FLOS ADONIS.

ADONIS was killed by a boar when hunting. Venus
who had quitted the pleasures of Cythereus for his sake
shed many tears at his melancholy fate. The fable tells
us that these were not lost, but mingling with the blood
of Adonis, the earth received them, and forthwith sprang
up a light plant covered with purple flowers. Brilliant and
transient flowers ; alas ! too faithful emblems of the pleasures of life ! you were consecrated by the same beauty
as the symbol of sorrowful remembrances.

Look, in the garden blooms the flos adonis,
And memory keeps of him who rashly died,
Thereafter changed by Venus, weeping, to this flower.

ANON.

BY this the boy, that by her side lay kill'd,
Was melted like a vapour from her sight ;
And in his blood, that on the ground lay spill'd,
A purple flower sprang up, chequer'd with white.

SHAKSPEARE

CERTAIN plants possess the remarkable property of opening and shutting their flowers at particular seaso s. Some, for example, open them all day, while others expand them only in the evening. There are likewise noctiflorous plants, which close their flowers in the morning.

In the above cases the degree of heat might be alleged as the exciting cause of the expansion of flowers; but this will not hold good with regard to other vegetables, which open and shut their blossoms at stated hours of the day, or at certain distances of time before change of weather. In these latter cases we must look for some other cause of the phenomenon, perhaps to some electrical changes in the state of the atmosphere.

Linnæus has enumerated forty-six flowers which possess this kind of sensibility: he divides them into three classes. 1. Meteoric Flowers, which less accurately observe the hour of folding, but are expanded sooner or later according to the cloudiness, moisture, or pressure of the atmosphere. 2. Tropical Flowers, that open in the morning and close before evening every day, but the hour of their expanding becomes earlier or later as the length of the day increases or decreases. 3. Equinoctial Flowers, which open at a certain and exact hour of the day, and for the most part close at another determinate hour.

T.HE DIAL OF FLOWERS.*

MRS. HEMANS.

'T was a lovely thought to mark the hours
  As they floated in light away,
By the opening and the folding flowers
  That laugh to the summer's day.

Thus had each moment its own rich hue;
  And its graceful cup or bell,
In whose colour'd vase might sleep the dew,
  Like a pearl in an ocean-shell.

'To such sweet signs might the time have flow d
  In a golden current on,
Ere from the garden, man's first abode,
  The glorious guests were gone.

So might the days have been brightly told—
  Those days of song and dreams,
When shepherds gather'd their flocks of old,
  By the blue Arcadian streams.

So in those isles of delight, that rest
  Far off in a breezeless main,
Which many a bark with a weary guest,
  Hath sought, but still in vain.

---

* This dial is said to have been formed by Linnœus. It marked
the hours by the opening and closing, at regular intervals, of the
flowers arranged in it

Yet is not life, in its real flight,
  Mark'd thus — even thus — on earth,
By the closing of one hope's delight,
  And another's gentle birth?

Oh! let us live, so that flower by flower,
  Shutting in turn, may leave
A lingerer still for the sun-set hour,
  A charm for the shaded eve.

ON FLORA'S HOROLOGE.

C. SMITH.

In every copse and shelter'd dell,
  Unveil'd to the observant eye,
Are faithful monitors, who tell
  How pass the hours and seasons by.

The green-robed children of the Spring
  Will mark the periods as they pass;
Mingle with leaves Time's feather'd wing,
  And bind with flowers his silent glass.

Mark where transparent waters glide,
  Soft flowing o'er their tranquil bed;
There, cradled on the dimpling tide,
  Nymphæa rests her lovely head.

But, conscious of the earliest beam,
  She rises from her humid nest,
And sees reflected in the stream
  The virgin whiteness of her breast.

Till the bright Day-star to the west
  Declines, in Ocean's surge to lave;
Then, folded in her modest vest,
  She slumbers on the rocking wave.

See Hieracium's various tribe
  Of plumy seed and radiate flowers:—
The course of Time their blooms describe.
  And wake or sleep appointed hours.

Broad o'er its imbricated cup
  The Goatsbeard spreads its golden rays
But shuts its cautious petals up,
  Retreating from the noontide blaze.

Pale as a pensive cloister'd nun,
  The Bethlem Star her face unveils,
When o'er the mountain peers the Sun,
  But shades it from the vesper gales.

Among the loose and arid sands
  The humble Arenaria creeps;
Slowly the Purple Star expands,
  But soon within its calyx sleeps.

And those small bells so lightly ray'd
  With young Aurora's rosy hue,
Are to the noontide Sun display'd,
  But shut their plaits against the dew.

On upland slopes the shepherds mark
  The hour, when, as the dial true,
Cichorium to the towering Lark
  Lifts her soft eyes, serenely blue.

And thou, "Wee crimson-tipped flower,"
  Gatherest thy fringed mantle round
Thy bosom, at the closing hour,
  When nightdrops bathe the turfy ground.

Unlike Silene, who declines
  The garish noontide's blazing light,
But when the evening crescent shines,
  Gives all her sweetness to the night.

Thus in each flower and simple bell,
  That in our path betrodden lie,
Are sweet remembrancers, who tell
  How fast their winged moments fly.

THE DIRGE OF FLOWERS

MRS. HEMANS.

Bring flowers to the captive's lonely cell, —
They have tales of the joyous woods to tell,
Of the free blue streams and the glowing sky,
And the bright world shut from his languid eye,
They will bear him a thought of the sunny hours,
And a dream of his youth — bring flowers, wild flowers

Bring flowers, fresh flowers, for the bride to wear,
They were born to blush on her shining hair:
She is leaving the home of her childish mirth,
She has bid farewell to her father's hearth,
Her place is now by another's side; —
Bring flowers for the locks of the fair young bride.

Bring flowers, pale flowers, o'er the bier to shed, —
A crown for the brow of the early dead.
For this through its leaves has the white Rose burst,
For this in the woods was the Violet nurst:
Though they smile in vain for what once was ours,
They are love's *last* gift — bring flowers, pale flowers.

Bring flowers to the shrine where we kneel in prayer, —
They are nature's off'ring, their place is there:
They speak of hope to the fainting heart;
With the voice of promise they come and part;
They sleep in dust through the wintry hours;
Then break forth in glory : — bring flowers, bright flowers

AUTUMN FLOWERS.

STRICKLAND.

FLOWERS of the closing year!
  Ye bloom amidst decay,
And come like friends sincere,
When wintry storms appear,
  And all have pass'd away
That clothed gay spring's luxuriant bowers,
With garlands meet for sunny hours.

When Rose and Lily fade,
  And later Amaranths fail,
And leaves in grove and glade
Assume a russet shade,
  And shiver in the gale,
Or, withering, strew the chilly plain
With blighted hopes of summer's reign. —

'Tis then, when sternly lours,
  O'er Nature's changing face,
Dark clouds and drifting showers,
Ye come, ye come, sweet flowers!
  With meek and touching grace;
And o'er the parting season's wing
A wreath of lingering beauty fling.

The Harebell, bright and blue,
  That loves the dingle wild,
    20*

In whose cerulean hue
Heaven's own blest tint we view,
　　On days serene and mild;
How beauteous, like an azure gem,
She droopeth from her graceful stem!

The Foxglove's purple bell,
　　On bank and upland plain;
The scarlet Pimpernel;
And Daisy in the dell,
　　That kindly blooms again
When all her sisters of the spring
On earth's cold lap are withering.

The bine-weed, pure and pale,
　　That sues to all for aid;
And, when rude storms assail,
Her snowy virgin veil
　　Doth, like some timid maid,
In conscious weakness most secure,
Unscathed its sternest shocks endure

How fair her pendent wreath
　　O'er bush and brake is twining!
While meekly there beneath,
'Mid fern and blossom'd heath,
　　Her lowlier sisters shining,
Tinged with the blended hues that streak
A slumbering infant's tender cheek

And there Vimiria* weaves
 Her light and feathery bowers,
'Mid russet-shaded leaves,
Where Robin sits and grieves
 Your hasting death, sweet flowers .
He sings your requiem all the day,
And mourns because ye pass away.

THE DEATH OF THE FLOWERS.

BRYANT.

THE melancholy days are come,
 The saddest of the year,
Of wailing winds, and naked woods,
 And meadows brown and sere.
Heap'd in the hollows of the grove
 The wither'd leaves lie dead;
They rustle to the eddying gust,
 And to the rabbit's tread.
The robin and the wren are flown,
 And from the shrub the jay ;
And from the wood-top calls the crow,
 Through all the gloomy day.

Where are the flowers, the fair young flowers
 That lately sprung and stood
In brighter light and softer airs, —
 A beauteous sisterhood ?

* Traveller's joy.

Alas! they all are in their graves:
    The gentle race of flowers
Are lying in their lowly beds,
    With the fair and good of ours.
The rain is falling where they lie;
    But the cold November rain
Calls not, from out the gloomy earth,
    The lovely ones again.

The Wind-flower and the Violet,
    They perish'd long ago,
And the Wild-rose and the Orchis died
    Amid the summer glow;
But on the hill the Golden-rod,
    And the Aster in the wood,
And the yellow Sun-flower by the brook
    In autumn beauty stood,
Till fell the frost from the clear, cold heaven,
    As falls the plague on men,
And the brightness of their smile was gone
    From upland, glade, and glen.

And now, when comes the calm, mild day,
    As still such days will come,
To call the squirrel and the bee
    From out their winter home,
When the sound of dropping nuts is heard,
    Though all the trees are still,
And twinkle in the smoky light
    The waters of the rill,

The south wind searches for the flowers
  Whose fragrance late he bore,
And sighs to find them in the wood
  And by the stream no more.

And then I think of one who in
  Her youthful beauty died,—
The fair, meek blossom, that grew up
  And faded by my side:
In the cold moist earth we laid her, when
  The forest cast the leaf,
And we wept that one so lovely
  Should have a life so brief;
Yet not unmeet it was, that one,
  Like that young friend of ours,
So gentle and so beautiful,
  Should perish with the flowers.

TO BLOSSOMS.

HERRICK.

Fair pledges of a fruitful tree,
  Why do ye fall so fast?
  Your date is not so past,
But you may stay here yet awhile,
  To blush and gently smile.
    And go at last

What ! were ye born to be
 An hour or half's delight,
 And so to bid good-night ?
'T was pity Nature brought ye forth
 Merely to show your worth,
  And lose you quite.

But you are lovely leaves, where we
 May read how soon things have
 Their end, though ne'er so brave :
And after they have shown their pride
 Like you, awhile, they glide
  Into the grave.

SENTIMENT OF FLOWERS

MEZEREON.—Coquette.

Well, well! adieu for ever,
  My heart has broken free;
I've brought myself to sever
  My pleasant tie to thee.

I blame myself for letting thee
  My better angel seem,
And forgive thee by forgetting thee,
  As some uneasy dream.

Farewell! enjoy the moments
  My rivals will think sweet,
And call it sunshine, if you will,
  That brings them to your feet.

They'll see the shades besetting thee,
  And learn my lesson yet,
To forgive thee by forgetting thee,
  Thou beautiful Coquette!

Farewell! with all thy brilliancy,
  Thy autumn will steal on,
And the sear and yellow chronicle
  Will write that it is gone.

Thy bloom will be forgetting thee
  When brightest it should seem,
And go like me forsaking thee,
  Like the color of a dream.

N. Y. Statesman.

ORANGE FLOWERS.—Bridal Festivity.

Bind the white orange flowers in her hair;
  Soft be their shadow, soft and somewhat pale,
For they are omens.   Many anxious years
  Are on the wreath that bends the bridal veil.

The maiden leaves her childhood and her home,
  All that the past has known of happy hours,
Perhaps her happiest ones—well may there be
  A faint, wan color, in those orange flowers.

For they are pale as hope, and hope is pale
  With earnest watching over future years,
With all the promise of their loveliness,
  The bride and morning bathe their wreath in tears.

L. E. Landon.

" I clasped the string of costly pearls,
    The gifts of courtship's hours;
I placed upon her shining curls
    The wreath of orange flowers.
O'er her sweet face I flung the veil,
    Yet drew it half aside,
That thy triumphant gaze might hail
    The beauty of thy bride."

PHEASANT'S EYE, OR FLOS ADONIS.

        Ay, do not fear
Thou'lt be remembered long,
The canker-worm of the heart
Is ne'er forgotten.

Mrs. Hemans.

COWSLIP.—Attractive Grace.

I would bring to thee a cowslip,
    My beautiful, my own,
Such a fair and modest flower
    Is like to thee alone.

L. H.

WHITE POPPY.—SLEEP OF THE HEART.

> SLEEP, heart of mine,
>   Why should love awake thee?
> Like yon closed rosebud.
>   To thy rest betake thee.
> Waken, heart of mine,
>   From such dangerous sleeping;
> Love's haunted visions
>   Surely end in weeping.
>
> MISS LANDON.

PERUVIAN HELIOTROPE.—DEVOTION.

> THOU wast that all to me, love,
>   For which my soul did pine;
> A green isle in the sea, love,
>   A fountain and a shrine,
> All wreathed round about with flowers—
>   And the flowers they all were mine.
>
> E. A. POE.

My love has never sought reward, 'twas joy enough for me
To pass my life in loneliness, and cherish thoughts of thee.

MRS. EMBURY.

> If to feel the deep devotion
>   Of a pilgrim at a shrine,
> If to weep with fond emotion
>   Be to love thee, I am thine.
> If to treasure every token,
>   Every look, and every sign,
> Every light word thou hast spoken
>   Be to love thee, I am thine.
>
> MRS. V. E. HOWARD

SENSITIVE PLANT.—DELICATE FEELINGS.

> HEARTS
> Whose beatings are too gentle for the world.
>
> WILLS

MYRTLE.—Love.

There is to youth one love,
   Intense, devoted, pure,
One dream, all other dreams above,
   Deep, passionate, and sure.
Its colors blend with every joy,
   In every hope are wrought;
It is the load star to the boy,
   His sole engrossing thought.
J. H. Bright

          Love will bear
What would weigh down an angel's wing to earth,
And still look heavenward.
L. E. L.

   " It is an ever fixed mark,
It is the star of every wandering bark,
It looks on tempests and is never shaken."
Shakspeare

We loved: our love was like a chord of music,
Such as the wind that sweeps a lute draws forth.
Meeting a passive echo from another.
It was a vision such as blessed spirits
Dream of in heaven, their earthly days recalling.
Halm

   The world that I had known went by
   As a vain shadow, on mine eye
      There rose a new and dreamful one,
   'Twas like the cloudy realms that lie
   Shadowy and brief, in Autumn's sky
      Before the setting sun.
Whittier.

I loved, as those love who but one image know
In the blue sky above, on the bright earth below;
I had not a thought in which thou hadst no part,
In the wide world I sought but a place in thy heart.
L. E. L.

WEEPING WILLOW.—Forsaken.

ALL that it hoped,
   My heart believed ;
And when most trusting,
   Was most deceived.

A shadow has fallen
   O'er my young years ;
And hopes, when brightest,
   Are quenched in tears.

MRS. JAMIESON.

But thou, where'er thy choice may lead,
   Unmindful of the wreck it makes,
One heart shall follow thee with prayer,
   And bless thee while for thee it breaks.

DA PONTE.

SORROWFUL GERANIUM.—Sorrowful Remembrances.

BUT can I answer back,
When all my thoughts are of the changed, the dead—
When I can feel no more the radiance shed
   O'er youth and hope's bright track ?
Alas ! thy looks but thrill my heart to meet
All the past glances that were once so sweet.

Farewell ! I love thy tone,
Thy cheerful smile, as one would love to see
The sunlight gilding river, hill, and tree,
   Though his own path were lone ;
But cast thy bright hopes on another's shrine,
They mingle not with drooping thoughts like mine.

L. H.

BUTTER CUPS.—Riches.

THOU'LT be so rich that thou shalt dine on pearls
   Breakfast on rubies, and on guineas sup ;
Yet all thy life the sport of laughing girls,
   And forced at last to give thy treasures up.

CROCUS.—Smiles and Cheerfulness.

Smiles on thy path, oh! let Joy chase away
The pale, shrouding cares that have darkened each day;
In the gleam of the sunshine let sorrow depart,
And the smile of the lip be the smile of the heart.

PRIMROSE.—Youth—Early Joys.

Fair Primroses, ye open like bright dreams
    Linked with the early promises of youth,
Breathing of Hope's soft hues, her sunny gleams,
    Whispering the heart sweet thoughts of joy and truth.

                                        L. B

GENTIAN.—Virgin Pride.

                        Once again
I see her, and she standeth in her pride,
With her soft eye enkindled, and her lip
Curled in its sweet resentment like a line
Of lifeless coral.

                                        Willis

LAVENDER.—Mistrust.

    Sweetest smiles may light our way,
    Yet their sunny beams betray;
    Softest voices thrill our heart,
    And the welcome tones depart;
    While the love we thought our own
    Leaves us desolate and lone.

BLUE BOTTLE CENTENARY.—Delicacy.

    Such love there is in my heart for thee.

STOCK.—Lasting Beauty.

The charm of person doubly dear beneath the light of mind
                                        Whittier

TO AN AUTUMN ROSE.

TELL her I love her—love her for those eyes,
  Now soft with feeling, radiant now with mirth,
Which (like a lake reflecting Autumn skies)
  Reveal two heavens here to us on earth.
The one in which their soulful beauty lies,
  And that wherein such soulfulness has birth.
Go to my lady ere the season flies,
  And the rude winter comes thy bloom to blast—
  Go! and with all of eloquence thou hast,
  The burning story of my love discover;
  And if the theme should fail, alas! to move her,
  Tell her, when youth's gay summer flowers are past,
  Like thee, my love will blossom till the last!

CHARLES F. HOFFMAN.

Others! the world lies crumbled at my feet.
She was my all, filled up my whole of being,
Smiled in the sunshine, walked the glorious earth,
Sat in my heart, was the sweet life of life;
The past was hers, I dreamed not of a future
That did not wear her image.

FROM "LOVE,' A PLAY

" This is the torch upon the tomb of Love,
  Where like a sorrowing angel Hope must sit."

DAISY.—BEAUTY AND INNOCENCE.

Oh! beautiful upon his sight,
  Who bears a heart like mine,
Doth shine the soft unconscious light
  Of loveliness like thine.

A wearied man seeks not the smiles
  That brightly beam on all,
For dearer are thy simple wiles
  That only one enthral.

L. E

21*

DRAGON PLANT.—The Betrayer.

" Trust not thine own unaided strength
  To shield thee from his power."

Be sure
You credit anything the sun gives light to,
Before a man.   Rather believe the sea
Weeps for the ruined merchant when he roars
Rather the wind courts but the swelling sails
When the strong cordage cracks.

Rather the sun
Comes but to kiss the fruit in wealthy Autumn
When all falls blasted.   If you needs must love,
Forced by ill fate, take to your maiden bosoms
Two dead, cold aspics, and of them make lovers.
They cannot flatter nor forswear ; one kiss
Makes a long peace for all.

BEAUMONT AND FLETCHER

JOY.—Enduring Friendship.

It will wait,
Yea, pause for years before it dares to creep
To the embraces of the lonely tower,
Or storied pillar, but once twining there
It clings for ever, with its rich green wreath
Smiling against a sullen sky.

L. H

POPPY.—Oblivion.

Come, press my lips and lie with me
Beneath the lonely alder-tree,
  And we will dream a pleasant sleep,
And not a care shall dare intrude
Upon the marble solitude
  So peaceful and so deep.

H. K. White.

LILACH.—First Impressions of Love.

Spirit of Love, soon thy rose-plumes wear
The blight, and the canker, and sully of care;
Falsehood is round thee, Hope leads thee on,
Till every hue from thy pinions is gone;
But one bright moment is all thine own,
The one ere thy visible presence is known.

Miss Landon.

Oh, world of sweet phantoms, how precious thou art!

Miss Landon.

Oh, early love, too fair thou art,
For earth too beautiful and pure;
Fast fade thy day-dreams from the heart,
But all thy waking woes endure.

Mrs. Whitman.

MOSSES.—Ennui.

One word may read my heart,
And that one word is utter weariness.

Miss Landon.

There will come an eve to a longer day,
That will find thee tired—but not of play;
When thou wilt lean, as thou leanest now,
With drooping limbs and an aching brow,
And wish the shadows would faster creep,
And long to go to thy quiet sleep.

Willis

TULIP.—Declaration of Love.

I have a tale for thee; the Tulip's pride
Must tell thee with its rich and varied dyes
My dream of ardent love, for never yet
Have these same lips had power to whisper thee
How warm hath been my passion · take my flower,
And bid me breathe again.

WATER LILY.—Purity of Heart.

Beautiful water lily! thou art like
A young heart wakening in its purity,
To the first breath of Love.   Alone, alone!
What hath the mist and darkness of this world
To do with its bright leaves? a snowy gem,
It floats upon the bosom of the tide,
Like Love upon the course of this dark world;
Trembling and stainless guest! It looks to Heaven,
But from its spotless urn pours out such gifts
Of fragrant sweetness, that the passer by
Blesses the gentle vision, and beholds
In the fair flower an emblem of his dreams
Of early purity and silent love.

L. H

VIOLET.—Faithfulness.

Pale Violets, whose sweet breath has driven
    Back on my soul the dreams I fain would quell,
To whose faint perfume such wild power is given
    To call up visions only loved too well.

A. A. Watts

MYOSOTRIS PALUSTRIS.—Forget Me Not.

    "Oh love, forget me not,
Wear thou this flower for me upon thy heart;
There is a pure gift in its simple leaves
To cheer thy heart in sadness, and to sooth
The shadows that are round thee with a love
Unchanging, unobtrusive, and devout."   L. H

SNOW-DROP.—Consolation—Adventurous Friendship.

    Cherish this flower! is it not,
        Bright comer in adversity,
    Like one who braves a stormy .ot,
        To bear the torch of Hope to thee?

L. H

WALL-FLOWER.—FIDELITY IN MISFORTUNE.

THE task befits thee well,
To gather firmness as the tempests swell
Around me still, companion, wife, and friend,
To cling in fond endurance to the end.

VICTOR HUGO.

ALMOND.—HEEDLESSNESS.

I DO commit me to the unfriendly world
In the first beauty of my morning prime,
With a true heart all heedless of the storm,
Yet blushing brightly at the daring chance.

L. H.

NIGHT-BLOOMING CEREUS.—WEALTH OF TRUE AFFECTION.

SUCH is my love for thee, a hidden dream
In the bright day of thy prosperity,
Alone its pure and fragrant buds shall gleam
In the deep night of thine adversity.

L. H.

HONEY-SUCKLE.—SWEETNESS OF DISPOSITION.

THY gentle smile hath won me,
Oh, more than beauty's glow
Is the soft radiance of the heart,
Like Heaven upon thy brow.   L. H.

DANDELION.—ORACLE.

"MUCH the wonder grew
That one small head could carry all he knew."

GOLDSMITH

ROSEMARY.—REMEMBRANCE.

BE there one word for a talisman,
For ever 'twixt thee and me,
A spell to conjure pleasant dreams,
That word is Constancy.

L. H.

AMARANTH.—Unfading Love.

Is not our love unchanging ? let us wreath
The deathless Amaranth to deck our brow,
And through all ills of this most stormy life,
Lift up our thoughts to that eternal clime
Where Love shall put off mourning hues, and glow
In the bright robes of immortality.

L. H

I love thee, yet I do not weep
    That thou art mine no more,
I mourn thee, yet my feelings sleep
    In silence as before.
A common loss might tears bewail,
    But not a loss like thine,
And words might soothe Love's fancied tale,
    But not a love like mine.

M. J. Jewsbury

SWEET PEA.—Departure.

Let me weave a wreath for thee,
Of the delicate sweet pea ;
With its winged petals bright,
Ever whispering of flight,
Like thy tone, I must depart,
Thrilling on my eager heart,
While thy glad return to me
Linked with parting still must be.   L. IL

HAREBELL.—Submission.

I shall not blame thee, I shall only die !

Hernani.

LILY.—Purity and Stateliness.

Pure art thou, Lily, in thy robe of snow,
Imaging queenly forms that round us glow
Beautiful spirits, linked with visions high,
Breathing the fragrance of their native sky.

L. H.

FLORAL DICTIONARY.

FLORAL DICTIONARY.

A.

Acacia. — Chaste Love.

Acalea. — Temperance.

Acanthus. — The Arts.

Achilla Millefolia. — War.

Aconite-Leaved Crowfoot, or Fair Maids of France — Lustre.

African Marygold. — Vulgar Minds.

Almond. — Heedlessness.

Aloe. — Acute Sorrow or Affliction.

Althæa Frutex. — Persuasion.

Alyssum, Sweet. — Worth beyond Beauty.

Amaranth. — Immortality.

Amaryllis. — Pride.

Ambrosia. — Love returned.

American Cowslip. — You are my Divinity.

American Elm. — Patriotism.

American Linden. — Matrimony.

American Star-Wort. — Welcome to a Stranger.

Anemone. — Sickness.

Angelica. — Inspiration.

Angrec. — Royalty.

Apocynum. — Falsehood.

Apple-Tree Blossom. — Fame speaks him great and good.

Asclepias. — Cure for the Heart-Ache.

Ash. — Grandeur.

Ash-Leaved Trumpet-Flower. — Separation.

Aspen-Tree. — Lamentation.

Asphodel. — My regrets will follow you to the grave.

Auricula. — Painting.

B.

Bachelor's Button. — I with the morning's le ve have of made sport.

Balm. — A cure.

Balsam. — Impatience.

Barberry. — Sourness.

Basil. — Hatred.

Bay-Berry. — Instruction.

Bay-Leaf. — I change but in dying.

Bay-Wreath. — The Reward of Merit.

Bears'-Breech. — Art.

Beech-Tree. — Grandeur.

Bell-Flower. — Constancy.

Belvidere. — I declare against you.

Bee-Orchis. — Industry.

Betony. — Surprise.

Birch. — Gracefulness.

Bird-Cherry. — Hope.

Bird's-Foot Trefoil. — Revenge.

Bearded Crepis. — Protection.

Black Poplar. — Courage.

Black-Thorn. — Difficulty.

Bladder Senna. — Frivolous Amusements.

Blue Bottle Centaury. — Delicacy.

Blue Flowered Greek Valerian. — Rupture.

Blue Pyramidal Bell-Flower. — Constancy.

Bonus Henricus. — Goodness.

Borage. — Bluntness or roughness of manners.

Box. — Stoicism.

Bramble. — Remorse.

Branch of Currants. — You please all.

Branch of Thorns. — Severity or Rigour.

Bryony. — Prosperity.

Buck-bean. — Calm Repose.

Bud of a White Rose. — A Heart ignorant of Love

Burgloss. — Falsehood.

Bundle of Reeds with their Panicles. — Music

Butter-Cup. — Childishness.

Butterfly-Orchis. — Gaiety.

C.

Cabbage. — Profit.

Calla, Æthiopica. — Feminine modesty.

Calycanthus. — Benevolence.

Canary Glass. — Perseverance.

Candy-Tuft. — Architecture.

Canterbury Bell. — Gratitude.

Cardamine. — Paternal Error.

Catesby's Star-Wort. — Afterthought.

Cardinal's Flower. — Distinction.

Catalpa Tree. — Beware of the Coquette

Catch-Fly. — Youthful Love.

Cedar of Lebanon. — Incorruptible.

Cedar Tree. — Strength.

Chamomile. — Energy in adversity.

Chequered Fritillary. — Persecution.

Cherry Tree Blossom. — Spiritual Beauty

Chestnut Tree. — Render me Justice.

China Aster or Chinese Starwort. — Variety

China or Indian Pink. — Aversion.

China Rose. — Beauty always new.

Chinese Chrysanthemum. — Cheerfulness under adversity

Cistus, or Rock Rose. — Popular Favour.

Cobœa. — Gossip.

Cock's Comb or Crested Amaranth. — Singularity.

Colchicum or Meadow Saffron. — My best days are past

Coltsfoot. — Maternal Care.

Columbine. — Folly.

Common Bramble. — Envy.

Common Cactus or Indian Fig. — I burn.

Common Fumitory. — Spleen.

Common Laurel in Flower. — Perfidy

Common Milfoil. — War.

Common Reed. — Complaisance.

Common Thistle. — Importunity.

Convolvulus Major. — Extinguished Hopes.

Convolvulus Minor. — Night.

Corchorus. — Impatience of Absence.

Coreopsis. — Love at first Sight.

Coriander. — Concealed Merit.

Coronilla. — Success crown your wishes.

Cowslip. — Pensiveness.

Cranberry. — Hardiness.

Creeping Cereus. — Horror.

Crocus. — Cheerfulness.

Cross of Jerusalem. — Devotion.

Crown Imperial. — Majesty and Power

Crown of Roses. — Reward of Merit.

Cuckoo-pink. — Ardour.

Cyclamen. — Diffidence.

Cypress. — Despair.

Cypress Tree. — Death and Eternal Sorrow

D.

Daffodil. — Deceitful Hope.

Dahlia. — Instability.

Daisy. — Innocence.

Damask Rose. — Freshness of complex.on.

Dandelion. — Oracle.

Daphne Odora. — Sweets to the Sweet.

Darnel, or Ray Grass. — Vice.

Dew Plant. — A Serenade.

Dittany. — Birth.

Dogwood, or Cornel-Tree. — Durability.

Double Daisy. — Participation.

Dragon Plant. — Snare.

Dried Flax. — Utility.

E.

Ebony. — Blackness.

Elder. — Zealousness.

Elm. — Dignity.

Enchanter's Night Shade. — Witchcraft.

Endive. — Frugality.

Eupatorium. — Delay.

Ever-Flowering Candy-Tuft. — Indifference.

Evergreen. — Poverty.

Evergreen Thorn. — Solace in Adversity.

Everlasting. — Never-ceasing Remembrance.

Everlasting Pea. — Lasting Pleasure.

F.

Fennel. — Worthy all praise.

Fern. — Fascination.

Fig. — Argument.

Fig-Tree. — Prolific.

22*

Filbert. — Reconciliation.

Fir. —- Time.

Flax. — Fate.

Flax-Leaved Goldy-Locks. — Tardiness.

Flower of an Hour. — Delicate Beauty.

Flowering Reed. — Confidence in Heaven.

Fly Orchis. — Error.

Forget-me-not. — True Love.

Fox-Glove. — South.

Frankincense. — The incense of a Faithful Heart.

French Honeysuckle. — Rustic Beauty.

French Marygold. — Jealousy.

Frog Ophrys. — Disgust.

Full Blown Eglantine. — Simplicity.

Full Blown Rose. — Beauty.

Fuller's Teasel. — Austerity.

G.

Garden Chervil. — Sincerity.

Garden Marygold. — Uneasiness.

Garden Ranunculus. — You are rich in attractions.

Garden Sage. — Esteem.

Genista. — Neatness.

Gilly-Flower. — Bonds of affection

Glory-Flower. — Glorious Beauty.

Goats' Rue. — Reason.

Golden Rod. — Precaution.

Gorse. — Cheerfulness in Adversity.

Grape, Wild. — Charity.

Grass. — Submission.

Great Bindweed. — Dangerous Insinuation.

Great Flowered Evening Primrose. — Inconstancy

Guelder Rose. — Winter or Age.

H.

Hare-Bell. — Delicate and Lonely as this Flower.
Hawk-Weed. — Quick-Sightedness.
Hawthorn. — Hope.
Hazel. — Reconciliation.
Heath. — Solitude.
Helenium. — Tears.
Hellebore. — Calumny.
Hemlock. — You will cause my Death.
Henbane. — Imperfection.
Hepatica. — Confidence.
Hibiscus. — Delicate Beauty.
Hickory. — Glory.
Hoarhound. — Frozen Kindness.
Holly. — Foresight.
Hollyhock. — Fecundity.
Honesty. — Honesty.
Honeysuckle. — Bond of Love.
Hop. — Injustice.
Hornbeam Tree. — Ornament.
Horse Chestnut. — Luxuriancy.
Houstonia. — Content.
Hoya. — Sculpture.
Hundred-Leaved Rose. — Grace.
Hyacinth. — Play or Games.
Hydranger. — Boaster.

I.

Iceland Moss. — Health.
Ice Plant. — You freeze me.
Indian Cress. — Resignation.
Iris. — Message.
Ivy. — Fidelity.

J.

Japan Rose. — Beauty is your only attraction
Jonquil. — Desire.
Judas Tree. — Unbelief.
Juniper. — Asylum.
Justicia. — The Perfection of Female Loveliness.

K.

Kennedia. — Mental Beauty.
King-Cup. — I wish I was rich.

L.

Laburnum. — Pensive Beauty.
Lady's Slipper. — Capricious Beauty.
Larkspur. — Levity.
Laurel. — Glory.
Laurel-Leaved Magnolia. — Dignity.
Laurestine. — I die if I'm neglected.
Lavender. — Assiduity.
Lemon. — Zest.
Lettuce. — Cold-Hearted.
Lichen. — Solitude.
Lilac. — Forsaken.
Lily of the Valley. — Return of Happiness.
Lime or Linden Tree. — Conjugal Fidelity.
Live Oak. — Liberty.
Lobelia. — Arrogance.
Locust. — Vicissitude.
London-Pride. — Frivolity.
Lotus-Flower. — Silence.
Love in a Mist. — Perplexity.
Love in a Puzzle. — Embarrassment.
Love lies a-Bleeding. — Hopeless not Heartless.

Lucerne. — Life.

Lupine. — Voraciousness.

Lychnis. — Religious Enthusiasm.

Lythrum. — Pretension.

M.

Madder. — Calumny.

Madwort, Rock. — Tranquillity.

Maize. — Plenty.

Mallow. — Sweet Disposition.

Mandrake. — Rarity.

Maple. — Reserve.

Marjoram. — Blushes.

Marsh Mallow. — Humanity.

Marvel of Peru. — Timidity.

Marygold. — Despair.

May Rose. — Precocity.

Meadow Saffron. — My best days are past.

Meadow Sweet. — Uselessness.

Mercury. — Goodness.

Mesembryanthemum. — Idleness.

Mezereon. — Desire to Please.

Michaelmas Daisy. — Cheerfulness in Old Age.

Mignonette. — Your qualities surpass your charms

Milk Vetch. — Your presence softens my pain.

Mimosa. — Sensitiveness.

Mint. — Virtue.

Misletoe. — Obstacles to be overcome or surmounted.

Mock Orange. — Counterfeit.

Monk's Hood. — Knight Errantry.

Moschatell. — Weakness.

Moss. — Recluse.

Moss Rose. — Voluptuous Love.

Mossy Saxifrage. — Maternal Love.
Motherwort. — Concealed Love.
Mountain Ash. — Prudence.
Mouse Ear. — Forget me not.
Mouse Ear Chickweed. — Ingenuous Simplicity.
Mouse Ear Scorpion Grass. — Forget me Not.
Moving Plant. — Agitation.
Mulberry Tree. — Wisdom.
Mushroom. — Suspicion.
Musk Rose. — Capricious Beauty.
Myrtle. — Love.

N.

Narcissus. — Egotism.
Nasturtium. — Patriotism.
Nettle. — Slander.
Night-Blooming Cereus. — Transient Beauty.

O.

Oak. — Hospitality.
Oats. — The witching soul of music, hers.
Oleander. — Beware.
Olive. — Peace.
Orchis. — A Belle.
Orange Flowers. — Chastity.
Orange Tree. — Generosity.
Osier. — Frankness.
Ox-Eye. — Obstacle

P.

Palm. — Victory.
Pansée or Heart's Ease. — You occupy my thoughts
Parsley. — Feast or Banquet.
Passion Flower. — Religious Superstition.

Patience Dock. — Patience.
Pea. — An appointed meeting.
Peach Blossom. — I am your captive.
Penny Royal. — Flee away.
Peony. — Bashful Shame.
Pepper Plant. — Satire.
Periwinkle — Pleasures of Memory.
Persimon. — Bury me amid Nature's Beauties.
Persicaria. — Restoration.
Peruvian Heliotrope. — Intoxicated with Pleasure.
Phlox. — Unanimity.
Pimpernel. — Assignation.
Pine. — Pity.
Pine-Apple. — You are perfect.
Plane Tree. — Genius.
Plum Tree. — Independence.
Polyanthus. — Confidence.
Pomegranate. — Foolishness.
Poppy. — Consolation to the sick.
Prickly Pear. — Satire.
Pride of China. — Dissension.
Primrose. — Early Youth.
Privet. — Defence.
Purple Clover. — Provident.
Pyrus Japonica. — Fairies' Fire.

Q.

Quamoclet. — Busybody.
Queen's Rocket. — You are the Queen of Coquettes.

R.

Ragged Robin. — Wit.
Red Bay. — Love's Memory.
Red Mulberry. -- Wisdom.

Red Pink. — Lively and pure Love.

Rhododendron. — Danger.

Rocket. — Rivalry.

Rose. — Genteel, pretty.

Rose, Acacia. — Elegance.

Rosebay Willow Herb. — Celibacy.

Rose Campion. — You are without pretension.

Rosemary. — Fidelity.

Rudbeckia. — Justice.

Rue. — Grace, or Purification.

Rush. — Docility.

S.

Saffron Flower. — Do not abuse.

Saffron Crocus. — Mirth.

Scabius. — Unfortunate attachment.

Scarlet Flowered Ipomœa. — Attachment.

Scarlet Fuchsia. — Taste.

Scarlet Geranium. — Preference.

Scarlet Ipomœa. — I attach myself to you.

Scarlet Nasturtium. — Splendour.

Scotch Fir. — Elevation.

Sensitive Plant. — Bashful Modesty.

Siberian Crab Tree Blossom. — Deeply Interesting

Silver Fir. — Elevation.

Small Bindweed. — Obstinacy.

Small White Violet. — Candour and Innocence.

Small White Bell Flower. — Gratitude.

Snap Dragon. — Presumption.

Snow Ball. — Thoughts of Heaven.

Snow Drop. — Consolation.

Sorrel. — Wit ill-timed.

Southern Wood. — Jest or Bantering.

Spanish Jasmine. — Sensuality.

Spider Ophrys. — Adroitness.
Spider Wort. — Transient Happiness.
Spiked Speedwell. — Resemblance.
Spiræ Hypericum Frutex. — Uselessness.
Squirting Cucumber. — Critic.
St. John's Wort. — Superstitious Sanctity.
Star of Bethlehem. — The light of our path.
Stinging Nettle. — Cruelty.
Stock or Gilly-Flower. — Lasting Beauty.
Strawberry. — Perfect Goodness.
Striped Pink. — Refusal.
Sumach. — Splendour.
Sun Flower. — False Riches.
Swallow Wort. — Medicine.
Sweet Briar. — Poetry.
Sweet Flag. — Fitness.
Sweet Pea. — Delicate Pleasure.
Sweet Sultan. — Felicity.
Sweet-scented Tussilage. — You shall have Justice.
Sweet Violet. — Modesty.
Sweet William. — Craftiness.
Sycamore. — Woodland Beauty.
Syringa. — Memory.

T.

Tamarisk. — Crime.
Tansy. — Resistance.
Teasel. — Misanthropy.
Ten Weeks' Stock. — Promptitude.
Thorn Apple. — Deceitful Charms.
Throat-Wort. — Neglected Beauty.
Thyme. — Activity.
Tiger-Flower. — For once may Pride befriend me.

Tree of Life. — Old Age.
Tulip. — Declaration of Love.
Turnip. — Charity.

V.

Valerian. — Accommodating Disposition.
Various Coloured Lantana. — Rigour.
Verbena. — Sensibility.
Vernal Grass. — Poor but Happy.
Vervain. — Superstition.
Venus's Fly Trap. — Deceit.
Venus's Looking Glass. — Flattery.
Vine. — Drunkenness.
Virgin's Bower. — Artifice.
Virginian Spider Wort. — Momentary Happiness
Volkamenica Japonica. — May you be happy.

W.

Wall Flower. — Fidelity in Misfortune.
Wall Speedwell. — Fidelity.
Walnut. — Intellect.
Water Melon. — Bulkiness.
Wax Plant. — Susceptibility.
Weeping Willow. — Melancholy.
Wheat. — Riches.
White Jasmine. — Amiableness.
White Lily. — Purity and Modesty.
White Mullein. — Good Nature.
White Oak. — Independence.
White Pink. — Talent.
White Poplar. — Time.
White Poppy. — Sleep of the Heart.

White Rose, Dried. — Death preferable to loss of innocence.

White Violet. — Purity of Sentiment.

Willow. — Forsaken.

Willow Herb. — Pretension.

Winter Cherry. — Deception.

Witch Hazel. — A Spell.

Wood Sorrel. — Maternal Tenderness.

Wormwood. — Absence.

Y.

Yellow Carnation. — Disdain.

Yellow Day Lily. — Coquetry.

Yellow Gentian. — Ingratitude.

Yellow Iris. — Flame of Love.

Yellow Rose. — Infidelity.

Yew. — Sorrow.

Z

Zinnia. — Absence.

A Belle. — Orchis.

Absence. — Wormwood.

Accommodating Disposition. — Valerian.

Activity. — Thyme.

Acute Sorrow. — Aloe.

Adroitness. — Spider Ophrys.

Afterthought. — Catesby's Star-Wort.

Agitation. — Moving Plant.

Amiableness. — White Jasmine

An Appointed Meeting. — Pea

Architecture. — Candy-Tuft

Ardour. — Cuckoo-Pint.

Argument. — Fig.

Arrogance. — Lobelia.

Art. — Bear's-Breech.

Artifice. — Virgin's Bower

A Spell. — Witch Hazel.

Assiduity. — Lavender.

Assignation. — Pimpernel

Asylum. — Juniper.

Attachment. — Scarlet-Flowered Ipomœa.

Austerity. — Fullers' Teasel.

Aversion. — China or Indian Pink.

B.

Bashful Modesty. — Sensitive Plant.

Bashful Shame. — Peony.

Beauty. — Full-Blown Rose.

Beauty always New. — China Rose.

Beauty is your only attraction. — Japan Rose.

Beneficence. — Potatoe.

Benevolence. — Calycanthus.

Beware. — Oleander.

Beware of the Coquette. — Catalpa Tree.

Birth. — Dittany.

Blackness. — Ebony.

Bluntness of Manners. — Borage.

Blushes. — Marjoram.

Boaster. — Hydranger.

Boldness. — Pine.

Bond of Love. — Honeysuckle.

Bonds of Affection. — Gilly-Flower.

Bulkiness. — Water-Melon.

Bury me amid Nature's Beauties. — Persimon.

Busybody. — Quamoclet.

C.

Calm Repose. — Buckbean.

Calumny. — Madder.

Candour and Innocence. — Sweet White Violet

Capricious Beauty. — Musk Rose.

Celibacy. — Rosebay Willow Herb.

Charity. — Turnip.

Chaste Love. — Acacia.

Chastity. — Orange Flower.

Cheerfulness. — Crocus.

Cheerfulness in Old Age. — Michaelmas Daisy.

Cheerfulness in Adversity. — Chinese Chrysanthemum

Childishness. — Butter-Cup.

Cold-Hearted. — Lettuce.

Complaisance. — Common Reed.

Concealed Love. — Motherwort.

Concealed Merit. — Coriander.

Confidence. — Hepatica.

Confidence in Heaven. — Flowering Reed.

23*

Conjugal Fidelity. — Lime or Linden Tree.
Consolation. — Snow Drop.
Consolation to the Sick. — Poppy.
Constancy. — Blue Pyramidal Bell Flower.
Content. — Houstonia.
Coquetry. — Yellow Day Lily.
Counterfeit. — Mock Orange.
Courage. — Black Poplar.
Craftiness. — Sweet William.
Crime. — Tamarisk.
Critic. — Squirting Cucumber.
Cruelty. — Stinging Nettle.
Cure, A. — Balm.
Cure for the Heart-ache. — Asclepias.

D.

Danger. — Rhododendron.
Dangerous Insinuations. — Great Bindweed.
Dauntlessness. — Thrift or Sea Pink.
Death and Eternal Sorrow. — Cypress Tree.
Death preferable to Loss of Innocence. — White Rose
    Dried.
Deceit. — Venus's Fly-Trap.
Deceitful Charms. — Thorn-Apple.
Deceitful Hope. — Daffodil.
Deception. — Winter Cherry.
Declaration of Love. — Tulip.
Deeply Interesting. — Siberian Crab-Tree Blossom.
Defence. — Privet.
Delay. — Eupatorium.
Delicacy. — Blue-Bottle Centaury.
Delicate and Lovely as this Flower. — Hare-Bell.
Delicate Beauty. — Hibiscus.
Delicate Pleasure. — Sweet Pea.
Desire. — Jonquil.

Desire to Please. — Mezereon.

Despair — Marigold.

Devotion. — Cross of Jerusalem.

Difficulty. — Black Thorn.

Diffidence. — Cyclamen.

Dignity. — Laurel-Leaved Magnolia.

Disdain. — Yellow Carnation.

Disgust. — Frog Ophrys.

Dissension. — Pride of China.

Distinction. — Cardinal's Flower.

Docility. — Rush.

Do not abuse. — Saffron Flower.

Drunkenness. — Vine.

Durability. — Dogwood.

E.

Early Youth. — Primrose.

Egotism. — Narcissus.

Elegance. — Rose, Acacia.

Elevation. — Silver Fir.

Eloquence. — Iris.

Embarrassment. — Love in a puzzle.

Energy in Adversity. — Chamomile.

Ennui. — Moss.

Envy. — Common Bramble.

Error. — Fly Orchis.

Esteem. — Garden Sage.

Extinguished Hopes. — Convolvulus Major.

F.

Falsehood. — Bugloss.

False Riches. — Sun-Flower.

Fame speaks him great and good. — Apple Tree Blossom.

Fascination. — Fern.

Fate. — Flax.

Feast. — Parsley.
Fecundity. — Hollyhock.
Felicity. — Sweet Sultan.
Feminine Modesty. — Calla Æthiopica.
Fidelity. — Wall Speedwell.
Fidelity in Friendship. — Ivy.
Fidelity in Misfortune. — Wall Flower
Filial Love. — Virgin's Bower.
Finesse. — Sweet William.
Fitness. — Sweet Flag.
Flame of Love. — Yellow Iris.
Flee Away. — Penny Royal.
Frozen Kindness. — Hoarhound.
Flattery. — Venus's Looking-Glass.
Folly. — Columbine.
Foolishness. — Pomegranate.
Foresight. — Holly.
Forget Me Not. — Mouse-Ear Scorpion-Grass.
For once may Pride befriend me. — Tiger Flower
Forsaken. — Lilac.
Frankness. — Osier.
Freshness of Complexion. — Damask Rose.
Friendship. — Acacia Rose.
Frivolity. — London Pride.
Frivolous Amusements. — Bladder Senna.
Frugality. — Endive.

G.

Gaiety. — Butterfly Orchis.
Generosity. — Orange Tree.
Genius. — Plane Tree.
Genteel. — Rose.
Glorious Beauty. — Glory Flower.
Glory. — Laurel.
Good Education. — Cherries.

Good Nature. — White Mullein.

Goodness. — Good Henry.

Gossip. — Cobœa.

Grace. — Hundred-Leaved Rose.

Gracefulness. — Birch.

Grandeur. — Beech Tree.

Gratitude. — Small White Bell Flower.

H.

Hardiness. — Cranberry.

Hatred. — Basil.

Heart Ignorant of Love. — Bud of a White Rose.

Health. — Iceland Moss.

Heedlessness. — Almond.

Honesty. — Honesty.

Hope. — Hawthorn.

Hopeless not Heartless. — Love lies a-Bleeding.

Horror. — Creeping Cereus.

Hospitality. — Oak.

Humanity. — Marsh Mallow.

I.

I am your captive. — Peach Blossom.

I attach myself to you. — Scarlet Ipomœa.

I Burn. — Common Cactus.

I change but in Dying. — Bay-Leaf.

I declare against you. — Belvidere.

I die, if I'm neglected. — Laurestine.

Idleness. — Fig-Marigold.

Immortality. — Amaranth.

Impatience. — Balsam.

Impatience of Absence. — Corchorus.

Imperfection. — Henbane.

Importunity. — Common Thistle.

Inconstancy. — Great-Flowered Evening Primrose.

Incorruptible. — Cedar of Lebanon.

Independence. — Plum Tree.

Indifference. — Ever-Flowering Candy-Tuft.

Industry. — Bee Orchis.

I ne'er shall look upon his like again. — Rhododendron.

Infidelity. — Yellow Rose.

Ingenuous Simplicity. — Mouse-Ear Chickweed

Ingratitude. — Yellow Gentian.

Injustice. — Hops.

Innocence. — Daisy.

Inspiration. — Angelica.

Instability. — Dahlia.

Instructive. — Bay-Berry.

Intellect. — Walnut.

Intoxicated with Pleasure. — Peruvian Heliotrope.

I with the morning's love have oft made sport. — Bach
    elor's Button.

I wish I was rich. — King-Cup.

J.

Jealousy. — French Marigold.

Jest. — Southern Wood.

Justice. — Rudbeckia.

K.

Knight Errantry. — Monk's Hood.

L.

Lamentation. — Aspen Tree

Lasting Beauty. — Gilly Flower.

Lasting Pleasure. — Everlasting Pea.

Liberty. — Live Oak.

Life. — Lucerne.

Levity. — Larkspur.

Lively and Pure Love. — Red Pink.

Love. — Myrtle.

Love at first sight. — Coreopsis.

Love returned. — Ambrosia.

Love's memory. — Red Bay.

Love Match, A. — London Pride.

Lustre. — Aconite-Leaved Crowfoot.

Luxuriancy. — Horse Chestnut.

M.

Majesty and Power. — Crown Imperial.

Maternal Care. — Coltsfoot.

Maternal Love. — Mossy Saxifrage.

Maternal Tenderness. — Wood Sorrel.

Matrimony. — American Linden.

May you be blessed, though I be miserable! — Volk. amenica Japonica.

Medicine. — Swallow-Wort.

Meekness with Dignity. — Plumbago.

Melancholy Lover. — Weeping Willow.

Memory. — Mock Orange.

Mental Beauty.—Kennedia.

Message. — Iris.

Mirth. — Saffron Crocus.

Misanthropy. — Fullers' Teasel.

Modesty. — Sweet Violet.

Momentary Happiness. — Virginia Spider Wort.

Music. — Bundles of Reeds with Panicles.

My best Days are past. — Meadow Saffron

My Heart bleeds for you. — Camellia Japonica.

My regrets will follow you to the grave. — Asphodel

N.

Neatness. — Genista.

Necessitude. — Locust.

Neglected Beauty. — Throatwort.

Never-Ceasing Remembrance. — Everlasting.

Night. — Convolvulus Minor.

O.

Obstacle. — Ox-Eye.

Obstinacy. — Small Bindweed.

Old Age. — Tree of Life.

Oracle. — Dandelion.

Ornament. — Hornbeam Tree.

Obstacles to surmount. — Misletoe

P.

Painting. — Auricula.

Participation. — Double Daisy.

Paternal Error. — Lady's Smock.

Patience. — Patience Dock.

Patriotism. — Nasturtium.

Peace. — Olive.

Pensive Beauty. — Laburnum.

Pensiveness. — Cowslip.

Perfect Goodness. — Strawberry.

Perfidy. — Common Laurel in Flower

Perplexity. — Lover in a Mist.

Persecution. — Chequered Fritillary.

Perseverance. — Canary Glass.

Persuasion. — Althæa Frutex.

Pity. — Pine.

Play. — Hyacinth.

Pleasures of Memory. — Periwinkle.

Plenty. — Maize.

Poetry. — Sweet Briar.

Poor but Happy. — Vernal Grass.

Popular Favour. — Cistus.

Poverty. — Evergreen Clematis.

Precaution. — Golden Rod.

Precocity. — May Rose.

Preference. — Scarlet Geranium.

Presumption. — Snap Dragon.

Pretension. — Lythrum.
Pride. — Amaryllis.
Profit. — Cabbage.
Prolific. — Fig Tree.
Promptitude. — Ten Weeks' Stock.
Prosperity. — Bryony.
Protection. — Bearded Crepis.
Provident. — Purple Clover.
Prudence. — Mountain Ash.
Purification or Grace. — Rue.
Purity and Modesty. — White Lily.
Purity of Sentiment. — White Violet.

Q.

Quick Sightedness. — Hawkweed.

R.

Rarity. — Mandrake.
Reason. — Goat's Rue.
Recluse. — Moss.
Reconciliation. — Filbert.
Refusal. — Striped Pink.
Religious Enthusiasm. — Lychnis.
Religious Superstition. — Passion-Flower
Remorse. — Bramble.
Render me Justice. — Chestnut Tree.
Resemblance. — Spiked Speedwell.
Reserve. — Maple.
Resignation. — Indian Cress.
Resistance. — Tansy.
Restoration. — Persicaria.
Return of Happiness. — Lily of the Valley
Revenge. — Bird's-Foot Trefoil.
Reward of Virtue. — Crown of Roses.
Reward of Merit. — Bay Wreath.
Riches. — Wheat.   24

Rigour. — Various-Coloured Lantana.
Rivalry. — Rocket.
Royalty. — Angrec.
Rupture. — Blue Flowered Greek Valerian.
Rustic Beauty. — French Honeysuckle.

S.

Satire. — Pepper Plant.
Sculpture. — Hoya.
Sensibility. — Verbena.
Sensitiveness. — Mimosa.
Sensuality. — Spanish Jasmine.
Separation. — Ash-Leaved Trumpet-Flower.
Serenade. — Dew Plant.
Severity. — Branch of Thorns.
She will be Fashionable. — Queen's Rocket.
Slander. — Nettle.
Sleep of the Heart. — White Poppy.
Sickness. — Anemone.
Silence. — Lotus Flower.
Simplicity. — Full-Blown Eglantine.
Sincerity. — Garden Chervil.
Singularity. — Crested Amaranth.
Snare. — Dragon Plant.
Solace in Adversity. — Evergreen Thorn.
Solitude. — Heath.
Sorrow. — Yew.
Sourness. — Barberry.
Spiritual Beauty. — Cherry Tree Blossom
Splendour. — Scarlet Nasturtium.
Spleen. — Common Fumitory.
Stoicism. — Box.
Strength — Cedar Tree.
Submission — Grass.
Success crown your wishes. — Coronilla.
Superstition. — Vervain.
Superstitious Sanctity. — St. John's Wort.
Surprise. — Betony.
Susceptibility. — Wax Plant.

Suspicion. — Mushroom.
Sweet Disposition. — Mallow.
Sweets to the Sweet. — Daphne Odora.

T.

Talent. — White Pink.
Tardiness. — Flax-Leaved Goody-Locks.
Taste. — Scarlet Fuchsia.
Tears. — Helenium.
Temperance. — Asalea.
The Arts. — Acanthus.
The incense of a Faithful Heart. — Frankincense.
The light of our path. — Star of Bethlehem.
The perfection of human loveliness. — Justicia.
The witching soul of Music, hers. — Oats.
Thoughts. — Heart's-Ease.
Thoughts of Heaven. — Snow Bell.
Time. — White Poplar.
Timidity. — Marvel of Peru.
Token, A. — Laurentinus.
Tranquillity. — Madwort, Rock.
Transient Beauty. — Night-Blooming Cereus.
Transient Happiness. — Spider Wort.
Treason. — Whortle-Berry.
True Love. — Forget Me Not.
Truth. — Bitter Sweet Nightshade.

U.

Unanimity. — Phlox.
Unbelief. — Judas Tree.
Uneasiness. — Garden Marigold.
Unfortunate Attachment. — Scabius.
Uselessness. — Spiræ Hypericum Frutex.
Utility. — Dried Flax.

V.

Variety. — Chinese Starwort.
Vice. — Darnel or Ray Grass.
Victory. — Palm.
Virtue. — Mint.
Voluptuous Love. — Moss Rose.

Voluptuousness. — Tuberose.
Voraciousness. — Lupin.
Vulgar Minds. — African Marygold.

W.

War. — Common Milfoil.
Weakness. — Moschatell.
Welcome to a Stranger. — American Starwort
Widowhood. — Sweet Sultan.
Winter. — Guelder Rose.
Wisdom. — Mulberry Tree.
Writ. — Ragged Robin.
Wit ill-timed. — Sorrel.
Witchcraft. — Enchanted Nightshade.
Woodland Beauty. — Sycamore.
Worth beyond Beauty. — Alyssum, Sweet
Worthy all Praise. — Fennel.

Y.

You are my Divinity. — American Cowslip.
You are perfect. — Pine Apple.
You are rich in Attractions. — Garden Ranunculus.
You are the Queen of Coquettes. — Queen's Rocket
You are without Pretension. — Rose Campion.
You freeze me. — Ice Plant.
You please all. — Branch of Currants.
Your presence softens my pain. — Milk Vetch.
Your Qualities surpass your charms. — Mignonette
You shall have Justice. — Sweet-Scented Tussilage.
Youth. — Fox-Glove.
Youthful Love. — Catch-Fly.
You will cause my Death. — Hemlock.

Z.

Zealousness. — Elder.
Zest. — Lemon.

BOTANICAL INTRODUCTION.

GENERAL ACCOUNT OF BOTANICAL TERMS.

On the outside of many flowers is seen a little green cup, which is called by botanists the *calyx*. The primrose, pink, and rose, give examples for analysis.

Within this flower-cup or calyx, which may be cut off to show what it contains, is seen the colored part of the flower, that part which is yellow in the primrose, blue in the violet, and red in the rose. The colored part is generally called the flower, or blossom; a botanist calls it the *corolla*.

The blossom or corolla may now be cut off, which in the primrose will be found to be of one piece, while in the rose and other flowers, it is composed of several parts or flower-leaves. These flower-leaves are called by botanists *petals*.

Within the flower-leaf or petal in most flowers, as in the primrose and lily, are seen several small thread-like organs standing round in a circle. These are called *stamens*.

Each stamen is composed of two parts, one long and slender called the *filament* or stalk; the other part, called the *anther*, is a kind of knob like a little box at the top, which when the flower comes to maturity, opens and throws out a colored dust called the *pollen*.

When the calyx, corolla, and the stamens, are all cut away, the centre part of the flower alone will remain on the top of the stem. This central organ is called the *pistil;* this consists of three parts, the top, which is called the *stigma*, the slender filament which bears the stigma is denominated the *style*, and the base is called the *germe*.

The *receptacle* is the end of the stem, where all the other parts of a flower are inserted.

The *pericarp* is the germe in a matured state; the name is derived from the Greek term *peri*, around, and *karpos*, fruit, denoting that it surrounds the fruit or seed.

These seven parts constitute what are called the organs of fructification, viz :—

Calyx, the cup.

Corolla, the blossom.

Stamens, organs within the corolla.

Pistil, the central organ.

Pericarp, containing seeds.

Seed, rudiment of a plant.

Receptacle, top of the stem.

Beside these principal organs there is often found attached to many flowers, a small appendage which is called the leaf-scale.

We will now give a short account of the classes and orders into which plants are divided, following the system of Linnæus, in preference to that of Jussieu. The first classes depend mostly upon the number of the stamens, viz :—

1st class. Monandria, or one stamen; this class contains the arrowroot, ginger, and samphire.

2d class. Diandria, or two stamens; for examples, we would name the lilac or syringa, the jasmine, sage, veronica.

3d class. Triandria, or three stamens; the grasses belong to this class, as also the crocus, iris or fleur-de-lis, and holly.

4th class. Tetrandria, or four stamens, containing the *houstonia cærulæ*, madder, and silver-tree, an exotic.

5th class. Pentandria, or five stamens; this class contains a great number of plants, many of them very beautiful, others quite poisonous; in the first division we name the forget-me-not, the trumpet honey-suckle, and the convolvulus; in the second division, known by their lurid smell and hairy stamens, the poison hemlock, deadly nightshade, and datura stramonium.

6th class. Hexandria, six stamens, presents us with the lily the tulip, crown imperial, and Solomon's seal.

7th class. Heptandria, or seven stamens, contains the horse chestnut, and the winter-green or chickweed.

8th class. Octandria, or eight stamens, gives us the *fuchsia* or ladies' ear-drop, heath, and evening primrose.

9th class. Enneandria, or nine stamens, the camphor. sassa-fras, and the bay (laurus nobilis), sometimes called pacifera, as sung by the ancient poets.

10th. Decandria, or ten stamens; this class includes the pink, the wild indigo, the wild pea, pokeweed, hydrangea, and Indian redbud.

11th class. Icosandria; th ᵒ class does not depend on the number of the stamens, but ɔon the manner of insertion upon the calyx; " in this class we find the night-blooming cereus, a species of cactus, having very large flowers, with the calyx yellow, and the petals white; they begin to open soon after the setting of the sun, and close before its rising, never again to blossom. The most beautiful flower among the cactus family is said to be the cactus speciossissimus, with flowers of the color of crimson-velvet, more superb than even the grandiflorus. No class can offer more beautiful specimens than the Icosan-dria, if we look only at the cactus order, destitute in general of leaves, but with the stems often appearing like a series of thick fleshy leaves, one growing from the top of the other, and sometimes composed of a stem resembling flattened leaves, as the prickly-pear." In this class is also found the hawthorn, the strawberry, and the whole family of roses.

12th class. Polyandria; this has stamens separate from the calyx, and attached to the top of the flower-stem, as the magnolia, the tulip-tree, the pond-lily, the poppy, and the tea-plant.

13th class. Didynamia; this class is distinguished by the length and number of the stamens — four in number, two longer than the other, the wall-flower, and the foxglove, and trumpet-flower.

14th class. Tetradynamia, possesses six stamens, four short

er than the other two. Pepper, radish, and mustard, are in this class.

15th class. Monadelphia or one brotherhood; in this class we include all such plants as have their filaments united into one set. The fifth order of this class contains the genus passiflora or passion-flower; the seventh order contains pelargonium, and includes the genus geranium; the thirteenth order malvacæ, includes those flow rs whose stamens are united in a column, as the hollyhock, camellia japonica, mallow, and cotton.

16th class. Diadelphia, two brotherhoods; this class includes all those flowers which have their filaments united into two sets. The flowers of this class are called papilionaceous or butterfly-shape, as the bean and the pea. When these flowers contain ten separate stamens, even if papilionaceous, it is placed in the 10th class, Decandria. But this is a point difficult to ascertain, as in the pea for instance, it is necessary to take a pin and separate the filament which is alone, in order to perceive that it is not united to the other nine. This class contains the fumaria, Seneca snakeroot, and the whole family of plants with leguminous pods.

17th class. Syngenesia; this comprises a great number of plants. The essential marks of this class consist in the *union of anthers;* this gives a compound character to the flowers, making each plant a collection of little florets, placed upon the same receptacle, and within one common calyx; add to this the five stamens with their anthers united, forming a little tube. This class includes the marigold, the genus artemisia, the family of the asters, solidago or golden rod, and the genus chrysanthemum.

18th class. Gynandria. This presents an entirely new feature, which is the situation of the stamens upon the pistil, since the stamens appear to proceed from that organ In this class we find the orchis family, the ladies' slipper, and the milkweed.

19th class. Monœcia. This class Monœcia (one house), shows to us plants upon the same root, where we find some flowers possessing stamens, others pistils. The stamens are infertile and disappear without fruit, the pistils when fertilized produce fruit. The mulberry-tree, the amaranthus, the genus calla, one species of which gives us the Egyptian lily, a beautiful exotic.

20th class. Diœcia or two houses, has staminate and pistillate flowers upon separate plants. This order contains the willow or *salix*, the fig (ficus), mistletoe, so long held sacred by the Druids, and the more useful plants of the hemp and the hop.

21st class. Cryptogamia. This class includes all plants whose organs of fructification are too minute for our investigation, as mosses, ferns, lichens, and mushrooms. It may be observed that many of these plants whose flowers are invisible to the naked eye, present when viewed with a telescope a very curious and beautiful arrangement. It is said that Mungo Park, when once greatly discouraged by the difficulties which environed him on a distant excursion, was so struck with the providence of God, exhibited in the formation of the moss beneath his feet, that he resolved never to despair, knowing that the same beneficent care would be over all his creatures. In this same class we include the liverworts so useful in medicine, the algae or seaweed which swims upon the surface of the water, often covering it to great extent as the fucus natans, sometimes called the gulf-weed, which is very abundant in the gulf of Florida, and is found in various parts of the ocean, forming masses or floating fields many miles in extent. We must not omit the lichens many of them useful on account of their coloring matter, as letinus which is an excellent chymi-

cal test, and is obtained from the white lichen called orchal or
anchil. Nor should we forget the mushrooms, which present
numerous varieties, all held in much esteem.

We will now give a very brief account of the different
orders into which these classes are divided, but the student in
Botany, must consult a larger manual to gain an accurate
knowledge of these subdivisions. The arrangement of the
orders in the first twelve classes depend chiefly upon the number of pistils.

I MONANDRIA. Two Orders, viz:—
Monogynia, one pistil.
Digynia, two pistils.
For examples of the first order, we find the hippuris, a water-plant,
and ginger; for an example of the second, blitum, an American plant.

II. DIANDRIA   Three Orders, viz:—
Monogynia, one pistil; lilac, olive, salvia or sage.
Digynia, two pistils; sweet vernal grass, catalpa-tree.
Trigynia, three pistils; black pepper.

III. TRIANDRIA. Two Orders, viz:--
Monogynia, one pistil; fleur-de-lis, blue flag.
Digynia, two pistils; grasses, rye, oats.

IV. TETRANDRIA. Two Orders, viz:—
Monogynia, one pistil; plantain, dogwood-tree.
Tetragynia, four pistils; ilex or holly.

V. PENTANDRIA. Six Orders, viz:—
Monogynia, one pistil; mouse-ear, forget-me-not.
Digynia, two pistils; fringed gentian, parsley.
Trigynia, three pistils; snow-ball, elder.
Tetragynia, four pistils; grass of Parnassus.
Pentagynia, five pistils, flax.
Polygynia, thirteen pistils: yellow root or zanthorhiza.

VI. HEXANDRIA. Three Orders, viz:—
Monogynia, one pistil; tulip, lily, aloes, fan-palm.
Digynia, two pistils; rice.
Trigynia, three pistils; dock, sorrel.

VII. HEPTANDRIA. Three Orders, viz:—
Monogynia, one pistil; horsechestnut.
Tetragynia, four pistils; saurudus or lizard's tail
Heptagynia, seven pistils; septas, a native of Good Hope

VIII. OCTANDRIA.   Four Orders. viz:—

Monogynia, one pistil; evening primrose, willow herb
Digynia, two pistils; Feverfew.
Trigynia, three pistils; buckwheat.
Tetragynia, four pistils; this contains a rare plant called Paris, named after Paris of ancient Troy, for its remarkable beauty.

IX. ENNEANDRIA.   Four Orders, viz:—

Monogynia, one pistil; cinnamon, spice-bush.
Digynia, two pistils; dog mercury.
Trigynia, three pistils; rhubarb.
Hexagynia, six pistils; flowering rush.

X. DECANDRIA.   Five Orders, viz:—

Monogynia, one pistil; wild pea, rue, rhododendron.
Digynia, two pistils; pink.
Trigynia, three pistils; sponge.
Tetragynia, four pistils;
Pentagynia, five pistils; cockle, sorrel.

XI. ICOSANDRIA.   Three Orders, viz:—

Monogynia, one pistil; cactus, pomegranate.
Di-pentagynia, from two to five pistils; apple, pear
Polygynia, thirteen pistils; strawberry, roses.

XII. POLYANDRIA.   Three Orders, viz:—

Monogynia, one pistil; mandrake, pond lily, poppy.
Di-pentagynia, two to five pistils; piony, larkspur, columbine.
Polygynia, the thirteenth order, is divided into two sections, flowers with no calyx, and flowers with a calyx. In the first section is the virgin's bower, the anemone.

XIII. DIDYNAMIA.   Two Orders, viz:—

Gymnospermia, contains plants with four naked seeds, as lavender.
Angiospermia, plants with their seeds covered.

XIV. TETRADYNAMIA.   Two Orders, viz:—

Siliculosa contains plants with a short round pod, as peppergrass.
Siliquosa plants with long and narrow pods, as radish, mustard.

XV. MONODELPHIA.   Five Orders, viz —

Triandria, three stamens united into a tube; tamarind, blue-eyed grass
Pentandria, five stamens; passion-flower, stork-bill geranium.
Heptandria, stamens united; the genus pelargonium.
Decandria, ten stamens united; cranes' bill geranium.
Polyandria thirteen stamens united in a column; hollyhock, silk cotton-tree.

XVI. DIADELPHIA. Two Orders, viz :—

Peot-octandria, five to eight stamens ; fumaria longdalis.

Decandria, ten stamens in two sets ; Lima bean, licknries

XVII SYNGENESIA. Five Orders, viz : –

Equalis with perfect florets.

Superflua, disk florets perfect, rays pistillate.

Frustanea, rays neutral, disk florets perfect.

Necessaria, disk florets barren, rays fertile.

Segugata, each floret with a calyx.

XVIII. GYNANDRIA. Five Orders, viz .—

Monandria ; orchis.

Diandria ; ladies' slipper.

Pentandria ; milkweed.

Hexandria ; Virginia snake-root.

Decandria, wild ginger.

XIX. MONŒCIA. Six Orders, viz :—

Monandria ; breadfruit-tree.

Triandria ; sedge, zea mays (Indian corn).

Tetrandria ; mulberry-tree.

Pentandria ; amaranthus.

Polyandria ; corylus (hazelnut), arum.

Monadelphia ; cucumber.

XX. DIŒCIA. Seven Orders, viz :—

Diandria ; willow.

Triandria ; fig.

Tetrandria ; mistletoe.

Pentandria ; hemp.

Hexandria ; honeylocust, and green brier

Octandria ; poplar.

Monadelphia ; red cedar.

XXI. CRYPTOGAMIA. Six Orders, viz.-

First order contains the ferns.

Second order ; musai or mosses.

Third order ; hepaticæ or liverworts.

Fourth order ; algæ or seaweed.

Fifth order ; lichens.

Sixth order ; mushrooms.

CONTENTS.

25

274

CONTENTS.